As they ran, however, Greg felt an idea nagging at him. Something was wrong, although everything had happened so quickly, he couldn't determine what it was. He replayed spotting the assassin, Athos's tackling the king, the flight of the arrow . . .

Up ahead, in the woods, the would-be killer paused and looked back at them before continuing on. It was a mere split second, but it struck Greg as odd, as though the assassin wanted to make sure they were following.

And suddenly, Greg knew.

He thought back to the arrow the assassin had fired. It had landed in the ground behind where Athos had been, not the king. Which meant it hadn't been meant for the king at all.

It had been meant for Athos.

"Athos! Stop!" Greg cried. "It's a trap!"

The urgency in his voice froze the others in their tracks. They spun toward him, understanding on Aramis's face, confusion on the others'.

And then the attack came.

Also by Stuart Gibbs

THE LAST MUSKETEER

TRAITOR'S CHASE

STUART GIBBS

HARPER

An Imprint of HarperCollinsPublishers

Library of Congress control number: 2012011529
ISBN 978-0-06-204842-4

Typography by Erin Fitzsimmons
19 20 BRR 10 9 8 7 6 5 4 3 2
❖
First paperback edition, 2019

For Suz, Darragh, & Ciara

ACKNOWLEDGMENTS

I DID A GOOD AMOUNT OF RESEARCH IN THE SOUTH OF France for this book, and so I need to thank my wife, Suzanne, who accompanied me on that journey. It didn't take a whole lot of arm-twisting to convince my wife to join me on a trip to the south of France, but I think she would have preferred to spend more time exploring quaint little towns and less time exploring dark underground chambers or clambering about ancient Roman aqueducts in the rain. Thanks for being such a good sport, Hon.

In that spirit, I also need to thank my in-laws, Barry and Carole Patmore, for watching our children while we were away. This book wouldn't have happened without their help.

Finally, I'd like to thank my old friend Larry Hanauer, who first convinced me to visit many of the places in this book with him back when we were in college. If not for him, I might never have learned about the fascinating history of southern France, explored the Roman ruins of Arles, or descended into a cryptoporticus. Hopefully, dear reader, I can now pass at least some of that excitement of discovery on to you.

✦ PROLOGUE

Madrid, Spain
July 1615

THE ALCÁZAR, THE ROYAL PALACE, HOME TO THE KING OF
Spain and Portugal, was perched high on a hill above the
city. Like the Louvre in Paris, it had originally been built
as a fortress but was currently being converted to a more
pleasant place for the royal family to live—which meant
that, at the moment, it wasn't really pleasant at all. Despite
the blazing sun and summer heat, inside the castle it was
dark and cold. Michel Dinicoeur felt it was more like a
prison—and he knew prisons. He'd spent over a hundred
years of his life in one.

Michel was immortal. Long ago, he'd had grand plans to gain power and wealth. But things hadn't worked out the way he'd hoped, thanks to the Three Musketeers—Athos, Porthos, and Aramis—and Greg Rich. It had taken him centuries to recover from their meddling. Now he had a new plan—one that would not only allow him to get revenge on the Musketeers and Greg—but also provide him with even more power than he'd ever dreamed of.

Michel followed three guards through a maze of stone hallways and grand staircases until they arrived at the throne room. The decor was as drab as that of the Louvre, but Michel was surprised by the room's enormous size. Stained-glass windows allowed some sunlight to spill in, though the room was still so cavernous that torches were needed to fully light it.

King Philip III sat on a large wooden throne at the far end. He was only in his thirties, with a pointed beard and a twirled mustache. He wore what was considered extremely fashionable in 1615: bright yellow stockings, an ornately embroidered jacket, and a neck ruffle so large it looked as though his head was on a platter. Instead of a crown, a feathered hat was perched on his head. The look was supposed to inspire awe, but instead it made Michel think the man was a fool.

Unfortunately, Michel knew his own appearance was hardly impressive. He was dusty and weary from his long journey; his clothes were tattered and worn. And he was an invalid; there was only a stump where his right hand had once been, thanks to Athos's sword.

"Your Honor," he said in Spanish, as he passed between a gauntlet of armed soldiers and knelt before the throne. "Thank you for seeing me."

King Philip's eyebrows raised slightly in surprise. "You speak Spanish."

"You are surprised?" Michel replied, standing. In fact, he spoke five languages fluently—and could read and write another ten. When you were immortal, you had plenty of time for self-improvement.

"I didn't think any Frenchman was smart enough to master our language." The king's statement, though insulting, wasn't really unexpected. Every civilization in Europe thought itself better than every other.

"But the letter I sent you was in Spanish," Michel said. "As was your reply to me."

Philip shrugged. "I thought there might be a Spaniard helping you."

Michel did his best not to sigh. He had sent the letter with the aid of Milady de Winter, a handmaiden from King Louis XIII's palace. He had intercepted Philip's response en route, which was why he was here right now, prostrating himself before this pompous idiot. "Do you still possess what I inquired about?"

Philip smirked and reached beneath his silken clothes, revealing a chain of silver links around his neck. He tugged on it, lifting out a large black crystal that dangled from the end.

The Devil's Stone. Only one half of it hung on the chain, but there was something entrancing about it, as though it somehow wasn't of the earth.

Michel's heart pounded at the sight of it, though he fought to hide his excitement. The stone was the key to his plans. When both halves were combined, it had incredible powers. Long ago, it had given him the gift of immortality. More recently, he had used it to travel back through time, returning to 1615 from the twenty-first century with a plan to kill the Musketeers when they were only teenagers. However, Greg Rich had interfered. Greg was from modern times, and when he and his parents accidentally followed Michel back through time, they caused him to lose the Devil's Stone. Now Michel needed to find both pieces again. Fortunately, he knew where they were, as he'd tracked them both down once before, back when he had been known as Dominic Richelieu.

And yet, while he'd known this half of the stone was in the Alcázar, he hadn't expected the King to be *wearing* it.

Philip seemed to sense Michel's excitement and defensively closed his hand around the stone. "This must be of great value to you," he said, "to have come all this way for it."

"It is," Michel admitted. There was no point in being coy. If everything went according to plan, Michel would have this half of the stone again soon enough. "Though its worth is sentimental, not financial. Long ago, my family used to own it," he lied.

Philip gave a snort of laughter. "It must have been *very* long ago. This has been in my family for as long as anyone can remember."

Then you come from a long line of fools, Michel thought. *To have owned this for generations and never understood what it was.* But he replied deferentially, "That is correct, My Lord."

"And you have journeyed all the way from Paris hoping to get it back?"

"Correct again."

Philip laughed once more, but longer this time, as though Michel had told a joke. "Then I'm afraid you have wasted your time. I do not intend to sell this to you."

Michel bristled. "But in your letter to me, you said you might."

"That was when you were a man of power, a member of King Louis XIII's court." Philip held the stone up and smiled at it dreamily, as though entranced by it. "But things have changed. From what I understand, you were ousted from your post in the palace. You are now a fugitive, a traitor, and a pauper. Your only worth is the bounty placed on your head by the king of France. A bounty I am tempted to collect." Philip snapped his fingers and his soldiers swung their swords toward Michel. "So tell me, what could you possibly give me that could pay for this?" He dangled the stone tauntingly before Michel.

Michel didn't even glance at the swords aimed at his neck. Instead, he kept his eyes locked on King Philip's.

"I can give you France," he said.

PART ONE

THE ASSASSINS

ONE

Paris

GREG RICH CREPT SLOWLY THROUGH THE LOUVRE, clutching his sword tightly, fearing an attack at any second. Flickering torches lighted the rough-hewn stone walls as he made his way along the dirt floor. A rat scurried past him, no doubt to its burrow between the gaps in the stone, while clusters of bats hung from the high, shadowed ceiling. Although clad in his Musketeer's uniform—bright blue with the emblem of the king, a white fleur-de-lis, embroidered on it—the chill air made Greg shiver.

He was in the oldest section of the palace, a remnant

from when the Louvre was a fortress on the western edge of Paris. It was hard to believe this was actually part of the home of the king of France.

The bells of Notre Dame chimed in the distance. It was seven o'clock at night, and although back in the twenty-first century, it wouldn't have been late, here in the seventeenth, most people were already turning in for the night. The sound of the bells made Greg uneasy; two months before, he'd nearly been killed by Michel Dinicoeur in that bell tower.

As Greg edged through the dim corridors, he struggled to remain calm, practicing what Athos had taught him: breathe slowly, be alert to everything around you, keep your sword unsheathed so you're always prepared for . . .

Trouble. Bat squeaks and the flutter of wings alerted Greg that someone was approaching from behind. He spun, his sword at the ready, just as his attacker lunged from the dark passage. A blade glinted in the torchlight, clanging against Greg's own.

Greg took a swordsman's stance, right foot forward, and parried. Athos's lessons filtered through his mind. *Stay in the moment. Focus. No matter how hard he tries not to, your attacker will always signal what he's going to do next. Predict, prepare—and counter.*

Greg watched his opponent's hands and feet, guessed where the strikes would come next, and responded. They ducked and dodged, steel hitting steel. Still, Greg was on the defensive, forced to back down the passage as his attacker surged forward. But then, Greg saw his opening. He deflected a slash at his head, twirled to the right, and attacked.

His instincts were dead on. He had a direct shot at the heart. . . .

"Drop it," a voice hissed in his ear. Suddenly, there was another sword at his throat, cold metal biting against his skin.

Greg let his sword clatter to the ground.

"What'd you do that for?" the voice behind him asked, far less sinister this time.

"Uh . . ." Greg said. "Because you told me to."

"Why would you do what the bad guy tells you to?" The sword lowered from Greg's neck, allowing him to face the second attacker: Porthos. "After all, he's the bad guy. He's not looking out for your best interests."

"Well, what was I supposed to do?" Greg asked. "Out-duel two men while there's a sword pressed to my neck?"

"Yes." Athos—the first attacker—emerged from the shadows. "If that had been Michel Dinicoeur or Dominic Richelieu behind you, your head would no longer be attached to your body. How do you expect to catch the madmen if you give up so easily?"

"Maybe *you* can beat two men in that situation," Greg said. "But I can't."

"Then I'd recommend not getting into that situation,"

Athos replied coolly. "You should *always* be prepared for an attack from behind. No matter what."

Greg sighed and picked up his sword. Athos was right, of course. Which only reinforced the fact that, even after two months of training, Greg still felt way out of his league in a swordfight.

"Hey"—Athos put a reassuring arm around Greg's shoulders—"you're doing great. Honestly. If it hadn't been for Porthos, you'd have got me right in the chest."

"Yeah. I would have." Greg mustered a smile. "I almost did you in."

"Oh, I wouldn't say *that*." Athos thumped his hand against the metal breastplate concealed beneath his tunic. "This is *me* we're talking about. I still had a few tricks up my sleeve. But virtually anyone else, you would have beaten. You've come a long way in a short time."

Greg appreciated the praise, though he was also daunted by it. Sometimes he forgot this wasn't just for sport, like all those years of fencing lessons had been back in prep school. Now that he was a Musketeer, knowing how to handle a sword could be the difference between life and death. Especially when Michel Dinicoeur and Dominic Richelieu were out there somewhere, plotting against him.

It had been two months since Michel had sprung Dominic from the Bastille. The attack had come mere minutes after Greg and the others had been sworn in as Musketeers by King Louis XIII. Even though the Bastille was a massive protected fortress, it had proven little challenge for Michel. The guards had claimed Michel had used sorcery, rendering men unconscious with a mere touch and making the walls explode with a single incantation. Once free, both men had ridden north of the city and crossed the Seine—and when the guards had tried to follow, they'd been repelled by a fusillade of arrows, courtesy of René Valois, a staunch supporter of Michel and Dominic who had once been a leader of the King's Guard. By the time the Musketeers arrived on the scene, Michel and Dominic were long gone.

Greg still had no idea where they were, although he assumed they'd gone off to recover the Devil's Stone. Michel needed it to make his younger self, Dominic, immortal—for if Dominic died, then Michel would cease to exist. Greg wanted to find the stone just as badly as they did—perhaps more—for without it, he couldn't return to his own time. But now his enemies had a two-month head start tracking it down—and once they had it, Greg suspected he'd never get it back. He and his parents would be trapped in 1615 France.

Of course, there was always the possibility that Michel and Dominic hadn't gone after the stone at all but were merely lurking about Paris, waiting for the best opportunity to kill Greg and the Musketeers—a scenario Greg found equally unsettling.

Therefore, Greg had spent the past two months doing

two things: training with Athos and Porthos—or sleuthing with Aramis, the brains of the Musketeers. Aramis had gone out today to follow up on a lead, but Greg feared that this would end like all the others: nowhere.

"All right," Athos said, brandishing his sword. "Let's try this again, shall we? Porthos and I will set up another ambush. . . ."

"Another?" Porthos groaned. "Haven't we ambushed him enough?"

"Practice makes perfect," Athos replied. "Besides, it's not like we have anything better to do."

"*I* do," Porthos shot back. "A lady friend of mine needs an escort to a ball this evening. And she has some friends who could use escorts as well, if you're interested."

Greg glanced at Athos, thinking that a ball might be a nice change of pace from the endless training, but the young swordsman frowned. "There are deadly enemies on the loose," he said. "We have no time for dancing."

"I'll bet you wouldn't say that if Milady de Winter needed an escort," Porthos replied with a smirk.

Athos flushed red at the mention of Milady, though Greg couldn't tell if it was from embarrassment or anger—or both. "I have no interest in the queen's handmaiden," he snapped.

Before Porthos could reply, footsteps echoed through the passageway. The three boys immediately raised their swords.

A palace messenger boy rounded the corner and shrieked in fright upon seeing the three blades pointed his way.

"Sorry!" Greg said, lowering his sword. "Didn't mean to scare you!"

"It's my fault," the boy apologized. "I'm sorry, sir." He knelt and bowed his head reverentially.

Greg and the others had been getting a lot of this type of respect since becoming Musketeers. Greg found it a little creepy, although the others ate it up. Even Aramis, who felt that pride was a sin.

"What brings you to interrupt our training?" Athos asked the messenger.

"The king requests a presence with D'Artagnan," the boy replied.

After all his time in France, Greg was finally getting used to being called D'Artagnan. His real name was only known to Aramis, one of many secrets he was forced to keep.

"Guess you'd better make haste, then." Athos tried to sound light of heart, although Greg could hear the jealousy beneath it.

"All right." Greg sheathed his sword and followed the messenger down the passage. He could feel the others staring after him, wondering what King Louis could possibly want with him this time.

The messenger led him from the old fortress into the true palace. The dirt floors became wood, and the stone walls gave way to painted plaster. They passed through the section that housed the King's Guard, where Dominic Richelieu himself had once had an office.

Greg found himself wishing that he could tell his friends the truth about himself and where he'd really come from, but he knew he couldn't. How could he possibly explain that he wasn't from the distant town of Artagnan at all—but was instead from four hundred years in the future? Or that Michel Dinicoeur and Dominic Richelieu were actually the same person? Or that Michel was an immortal madman who'd traveled back through time to kill the Musketeers as revenge for something they hadn't even done yet? These were superstitious times, Aramis had warned. Greg's friends wouldn't understand. They'd think him a sorcerer or a madman or both.

Greg followed the messenger up a wide wooden staircase, and the Louvre suddenly became alive with activity. Greg had always assumed that the palace was only the king's home, but in fact hundreds of servants lived there as well—including the Musketeers themselves. The route took Greg right past their quarters. It was a small room and they all had to share it, but compared to the living conditions of most people in 1615 Paris, the accommodations were amazing. The boys all had beds to sleep on, rather than mere thatches of straw. And there was even indoor plumbing—as long as they didn't mind going down the hall and using a communal—and coed—bathroom that didn't have a lock on the door.

Greg's parents' room was right next door to his. King Louis had graciously allowed them to move into the castle as well after their rescue from La Mort. The door currently hung open, revealing that Greg's parents weren't in. Greg was wondering where they'd gone when Aramis burst out of the Musketeers' quarters.

"D'Artagnan!" he crowed. "Just who I wanted to see! You'll never believe what I learned today!"

"Actually, can it wait?" Greg asked. "The king asked to see me."

"I'll walk with you. It's too exciting." Aramis dropped in beside Greg and held up a tiny scrap of black fabric. It was two inches long, an inch wide, and torn on three sides—as though it had been ripped from a piece of clothing. "Remember this?"

"Of course," Greg said. "I found it."

The shred of fabric was the only clue the boys had to Dominic and Michel's whereabouts. A few months earlier, Michel had forced Milady de Winter to deliver a letter to a messenger at an inn. Under questioning later, Milady claimed that she had no idea what was in the letter or where the messenger was from—only that he was a foreigner. Aramis had believed her—but then, Aramis was smitten with Milady. Athos hadn't believed her at all—but then, Athos was also smitten with Milady, and he knew she liked Aramis more than she liked him.

The day after Dominic had escaped from prison, Greg

had asked Milady to take him to the inn. She had led all the Musketeers there on horseback. The inn only had a single room for guests, and there Greg had found the scrap of cloth snagged on a jagged splinter of wood that jutted from the wall. The innkeeper's wife said it *looked* like it was from the clothes the mysterious man had worn.

"It's silk," Aramis said proudly, as he and Greg followed King Louis's messenger through the palace.

"So?" Greg asked.

Aramis frowned. "Is silk not a big deal in the future?"

Greg thought about the clothes his family had owned. His mother had several silk dresses and his father probably had some silk ties as well. "I don't think it's cheap, but I don't think it's rare, either."

"Well, it's rare here. And expensive. Silk comes all the way from the Far East, and only a few shipments reach Europe every year. What arrives tends to stay in the port cities— usually Venice or Barcelona. Only the tiniest amounts of silk ever make it to Paris."

Greg stopped walking and examined the scrap of silk more closely. "So whoever Milady met at the inn that night was no common messenger?"

"Exactly. Anyone wearing such fancy clothes would most likely be the emissary representing the king of a foreign nation."

Greg's heart thumped in his chest. France was sur- rounded by countries that were always on the verge of invading: England, Spain, the duchies of Italy, and the Holy Roman Empire, which controlled Germany, Switzerland, and Belgium. If Dominic had dealings with *any* of them, it was reason for concern. "Which one?"

"I don't know yet." Aramis took the scrap of silk back and carefully tucked it away. "I need to figure out where this silk was made. I'll bet a month's wages that, wherever it is, Dominic and Michel have fled there."

"But we don't know that for sure," Greg said.

"No," Aramis admitted. "Still, this is the best lead we have."

"How long will it take to find out where the silk is from?"

"A few days—if we're lucky."

Greg silently cursed the backward age in which he was trapped. What would have taken five seconds to discover with a simple Wikipedia search could take *forever* to find out in the past. "There's no way to do it any faster?" he asked. "With every day that goes by, Michel and Dominic are getting closer and closer to . . ."

He caught himself at the last second, not wanting to mention the Devil's Stone before the king's messenger. Aramis recognized the worry in Greg's eyes, though. "Allow us a moment?" he asked the messenger, then pulled Greg into a small alcove where they could speak in peace.

"I know that finding the stone is of utmost importance to you," Aramis whispered. "I'm doing everything I can to figure out where it is. Over the past two months, I've combed through every book, scroll, and parchment in Paris. . . ."

"And you haven't found a single mention of it?" Greg asked. "There must be something somewhere. I mean, Michel had to learn about the stone somewhere, back when he was Dominic. . . ."

"Well," Aramis said hesitantly, "I did find *something* a few days ago. . . ."

"And you didn't tell me?" Greg couldn't contain himself in his excitement.

"It was merely an oblique reference," Aramis whispered, signaling Greg to keep his voice down. "It didn't even mention the Devil's Stone by name."

"What was it?"

"I found it in a scroll in the archives at Notre Dame. It was a transcript of the travels of a monk who stayed there two hundred years ago." Until Greg had met him, Aramis himself had been a cleric at Notre Dame, responsible for transcribing texts from one language to another. The cathedral had the largest library in the city. "He mentioned hearing about a magic stone with incredible powers that was last seen in the White City of Emperor Constantine."

"What's the White City of Emperor Constantine?" Greg asked.

"I don't know," Aramis admitted. "And neither does anyone else I've talked to. There were several Emperor Constantines in the Roman era, but they all lived more than a thousand years ago. . . ."

Greg felt all the excitement drain from him.

Aramis put a comforting hand on his arm. "Don't despair," he said. "We'll find the stone. I promise you that."

Despite his reassuring tone, Greg still felt hollow inside. "We *have* to," he said. "No offense, but I can't stay in this time forever."

"I know," Aramis told him. "I'm doing everything I can. . . ."

Before he could go on, the messenger coughed impatiently out in the hall. "Monsieur D'Artagnan. The *king* still waits for you."

Greg nodded, then told Aramis, "The sooner you can find out about that silk, the better. I'll take any lead I can get." He then followed the messenger down another hall to a set of large, imposing wooden doors flanked by two members of the King's Guard.

The messenger bowed subserviently before them. "At the king's request, I have brought Monsieur D'Artagnan."

The guards dramatically opened the doors and Greg passed into the throne room.

He had been inside it often—in fact, this was the very room he had landed in after jumping through time—and yet he never could get past how dull it was. It was so vast that the oil lamps barely made a dent in the darkness, though they did create a grimy slick of burnt oil on the walls and ceiling.

Louis XIII was slumped in his throne. The king was only

fourteen, like Greg. He'd taken the crown at the age of nine when his father was assassinated, and he still gave the impression of a young boy merely pretending to be king. His formal royal red gown, trimmed with ermine, swallowed him up.

"D'Artagnan!" Louis said. "Thank goodness you've come. . . ."

"I'm sorry it took so long, Your Majesty," Greg began. "I was practicing my sword-fighting skills all the way at the other end of—"

"I don't care about your tardiness. I care about my safety. I've just learned some terrifying news." Louis sat upright, his eyes boring into Greg's. "Someone in my family is plotting to kill me."

TWO

"AGAIN?" GREG ASKED THE KING. HE WAS ALL TOO USED to these paranoid outbursts. Louis was always concerned that someone was after him. "Who wants you dead this time?"

"My cousin Henry, the Prince of Condé," Louis replied.

"And how do you know he's plotting against you?"

"Why wouldn't he be? Until I was born, he was next in line for the throne. It's well known that he wishes I'd never been born."

Greg sighed. He'd given up trying to understand the

convoluted chain of succession to the French throne. "Do you have any proof that he's plotting?"

"Of course I have proof!" Louis stuck his nose in the air, as though offended by the question. "The captain of the guard reports that he heard a rumor to such effect while on patrol today."

Greg waited for more information to come, but none did. "That's all?"

"What more do you need?"

"Actual *evidence* of something would be nice. I hear rumors about plots to overthrow you all the time. . . ."

Louis turned even paler than usual. "You do? Do we need to increase the number of guards?"

Greg held up his hands, signaling the king to calm down. "No. What I meant is, all the talk doesn't mean anything. Your subjects love to gossip about palace intrigue, but they don't really know what's going on. The other day, I actually overheard someone on the street say that the *Musketeers* themselves were plotting against you."

Louis laughed. "The Musketeers! Plotting against me? You're my only friends in the world!"

"Exactly. It's ridiculous."

Louis nodded. "I apologize for my foolishness, D'Artagnan. It's just that being the king can be so . . . deadly."

"I understand." Greg knew the king's paranoia was actually well founded: there were plenty of people vying to wrest power from Louis—including his own mother, Marie de Medici, and, of course, Dominic Richelieu. Until the Musketeers had exposed Dominic, he had been one of Louis's most trusted advisers.

"I'm sorry to bother you with all this," Louis said. "It's just that . . . I don't really have anyone else to talk to about these things."

"And I appreciate that, Your Majesty," Greg told him. "Although, if you really need to discuss politics, Aramis knows much more about it than I do."

"Yes. I know he's very smart. . . ."

"And Athos knows more about military matters. . . ."

"He does, but . . ."

"And Porthos knows a lot more jokes than I do. . . ."

"True. In fact, he told me a very funny one the other day. But the thing is, D'Artagnan, you and I have much more in common."

Greg stared at the king, surprised. "We do?" The truth was, short of their ages, he didn't feel that he had much in common with Louis at all. Greg had originally thought being a teenage king would be awesome, but the reality was that Louis had lived an extremely lonely life, completely removed from society. He could often be clingy, petulant, needy, or imperious—and Greg far preferred to spend his time with the Musketeers.

"I've tried to figure out what it is exactly," Louis was saying, "and I think it's that we're both not really like everyone else here. I mean, I'm the king. And you . . . you're from so very far away."

You have no idea how far, Greg thought. In truth, Louis and everyone else (save for Aramis) thought he was from Artagnan, on the southern border of France near Spain. "I suppose you're right," he admitted.

"It's not easy being the king." Louis sighed. "Everyone *thinks* it is, but it's not."

It's a lot easier than being a peasant, Greg thought. Louis had everything he could possibly need, while the average person his age worked from dawn until dusk, ate gruel three times a day, and slept on a flea-infested thatch of hay. But instead, Greg merely nodded agreement.

"It's not just the people plotting against me," Louis went on. "It's the pressure of running the country. Plus I'm in charge of the army. And then I have to marry Anne of Austria in a few months just so our empires can have peace. I've never even met her!"

"Yeah," Greg said empathetically. "I can see how being forced to marry someone who doesn't even speak your language could be strange."

"Exactly!" Louis crowed. "Everyone else thinks I should be excited. But I'm not. I'm kind of . . . worried."

"I would be, too," Greg said. "You're only fourteen. People get married much later than that where I'm from." Greg spoke before he could stop himself, knowing what the next question would be.

"How late is that?" Louis asked.

"Around twenty," Greg lied. He'd once told Aramis that people in the future sometimes didn't marry until they were over thirty, to which Aramis had laughed and responded that people who were over thirty were almost dead.

"My goodness, how strange." Louis was silent, staring out a window for a moment. Greg followed his gaze as a large bird flew by. Louis sat up, suddenly struck by a thought. "Have you ever tried falconry?"

Greg looked at Louis, shaking his head. "No. I don't even know what it is."

"Really? See, that's what I'm talking about. You're such an outsider. Falconry is a sport—you take a trained falcon out into the countryside and then let it kill things."

"And then what?"

"That's it." Louis pursed his lips. "It's supposed to be more fun than it sounds. Kings have been doing it for centuries."

"It certainly sounds fun," said Greg, lying again. "But the thing is, I really need to spend my days working on my battle skills. . . ."

"Oh, pish. All work and no play makes D'Artagnan a dull boy. Porthos taught me that. You can certainly spare an afternoon. Let's say tomorrow."

"Could the other Musketeers come, too? It'd be good to have them around, in case anything dangerous happens,"

Greg said. "I mean, we'll be out in the countryside, away from the castle and all its protections. . . ."

Louis went pale once again. "I hadn't thought of that. I suppose you're right. Fine, then. All of us. Falconry. Tomorrow afternoon!" The king gave a pleased laugh.

Greg tried to plaster a smile on his face.

The doors suddenly opened and a guard announced, "Milady de Winter to see you, Your Majesty."

Greg swung around to see Milady standing at the far end of the throne room. Even in the torchlit gloom, she was radiant. Her golden hair and her bright blue eyes gleamed as though the sun were shining directly on her. She curtsied and lowered her head. "I beg your pardon, Your Majesty, but I have some details of your wedding to discuss."

"Very well," Louis said with a sigh. "I'll see you tomorrow, D'Artagnan."

Greg knelt respectfully, then headed for the door. Milady came toward him. As the future handmaiden to Anne of Austria, Milady served as the go-between on all matters of the wedding. She smiled brightly at Greg.

Greg went slightly weak in the knees. There was no denying that the girl was incredibly beautiful.

"Good evening, Milady." Greg tried to say it nonchalantly, but it came out sounding embarrassed.

"Good evening, D'Artagnan." To Greg's surprise, Milady caught his arm as she passed and whispered, "I need to talk to *you* as well. I've come across something of Dominic

Richelieu's that I think must be important."

Greg paused and looked back at Milady, but she continued toward the king. Greg had no choice but to leave, wondering what Milady had found. Unfortunately, he wouldn't be able to track her down and ask. Entering the maidens' quarters at the palace was highly improper. Which meant he'd have to wait for Milady to find him again and explain herself.

He expected he'd hear from her soon, however. There'd been something strange in Milady's voice. For the first time since Greg had met her, Milady had sounded afraid.

THREE

Greg exited the throne room, shaken by his brief encounter with Milady. He found himself alone in the palace; the messenger who had brought him there had doubtlessly been dispatched on another errand. Greg headed back toward his quarters, hoping at least one of the other Musketeers might be there. It would be nice to resume his conversation with Aramis, or to get a bit more practice in with Athos, or to have Porthos leaven his spirits with some jokes. As he passed his parents' room, however, he heard his mother call out, "Gregory. Is that you?"

Greg froze in mid-step.

"Mom, for the hundredth time, don't call me Gregory," Greg hissed. He hurried into her room and closed the door. "Everyone here thinks my name is D'Artagnan."

"Don't change the subject," his mother said. "Do you have any idea how late it is? It's eight-thirty at night!"

"But my curfew at home was eleven-thirty."

"That was in the twenty-first century! This era is far more dangerous after dark."

Greg rolled his eyes and was about to reply when he heard his father fumbling with the oil lamp by his bed. "Oh, what I wouldn't do for electricity!" Dad grumbled.

"Do you have a match, Greg?" Mom asked absently.

"*D'Artagnan*, Mom. And yes, I have two. But since they're the only two matches in 1615, I'm saving them for emergencies."

The oil lamp clattered on the floor. "Curse it!" Dad snapped. "I have to go find a candle." He hopped off his bed, then promptly slipped in the spilled oil and crashed to the floor.

Greg failed to cover his laughter as his father stormed into the adjoining room.

"Don't laugh at your father," Mom cautioned. "You know this hasn't been easy on us."

"Me either, Mom."

"You weren't the one who was captured and sentenced to death immediately upon arriving in this time. You weren't the one who was held in the world's most horrid, disease-ridden prison for three days. . . ."

"No, but I *was* the one who rescued you from there."

"I'm well aware of that. But it doesn't make what we went through any less difficult."

"I know." Greg lowered his eyes, feeling a bit ashamed. The truth was, as hard as things had been for him in 1615, they had been far worse for his parents. Their time inside the prison was traumatic. They had been treated horribly and forced to live in filth. Unaware that Greg was planning a rescue attempt—or that he was even alive—his mother had lost all hope. Even now, months later, she was still plagued by nightmares of her time in La Mort.

"The point is, we're worried about you," his mother said. "This time is dangerous enough as it is—and being a Musketeer is just asking for trouble."

"I understand your concern, Mom. But I need to be a Musketeer if I'm ever going to find your amulet again."

Greg's mother stared at him blankly. "What amulet?"

Greg frowned. His mother was also having memory loss. No matter how many times Greg explained it, she often forgot about the amulet.

"The one with the dark stone on a silver chain," Greg explained. "It had been handed down through our family for generations. The stone is one half of the Devil's Stone. And when the two halves are placed together, they give whoever holds them incredible power. A long time ago, the

Devil's Stone made Dominic Richelieu immortal and he tried to overthrow the king, but the Musketeers defeated him. They locked him away in the Bastille and separated the halves of the Devil's Stone. One half was given to Dominic's family to protect. That was ours. We're his descendants."

Greg's mother looked horrified; the memories were beginning to come back to her.

Greg continued. "Dominic ultimately escaped prison and spent centuries plotting his revenge. He changed his name to Michel Dinicoeur, found the other half of the stone, and then tricked you into giving him yours at the Louvre."

"Yes, I remember now. Michel offered to buy all our family heirlooms, and we needed the money. . . ." Mom paused, and a look of sadness came over her. "Oh Gregory, I'm so sorry."

Greg put his hand on hers and tried to sound reassuring. "It wasn't your fault, Mom."

"But I *did* give my amulet to that horrible man. And he did something with it. At the Louvre. Something incredible . . ."

Greg nodded. "The stone can turn any picture into a time portal. Dinicoeur did it with an old painting of the Louvre. But when he jumped through, we followed him. That's how we ended up here. In this time. Unfortunately, we now have to find both halves of the stone so we can go home."

"But how? There are no paintings of the future."

"True. But I have *this*." Greg reached into the small leather pouch that hung from his belt and removed his most prized possession: his phone. He'd kept it on him twenty-four hours a day for the last two months. "I have photos from home on this. If the Devil's Stone can turn a painting into a portal, maybe it can turn a photograph into a portal, too. This is our ticket home."

Greg's mother looked relieved for a moment—but then a worried look crossed her face. "Do you have any idea where this Devil's Stone might be?"

Greg shook his head sadly. "No. But Michel Dinicoeur does. Remember, he's already lived through this time period once. He knows where the stone is now, and he and Dominic have gone to find it. They need it to make Dominic immortal so that he can be rich and powerful for eternity. We need to stop them before he can do that. *That's* why I need to be a Musketeer, Mom. So I can track them down and beat them to the stone. So I can set things right and get us home again."

"Not necessarily." The words came from behind Greg, far quieter than his own, but somehow more powerful.

Greg spun around to see his father returning with a lit candle. He brought it to the bedside and perched on the mattress beside Greg's mother again. "You don't have to be a Musketeer to get the Devil's Stone back," he said. "I'm sure the other three could get it for us."

"I can't do that!" Greg protested. "I'm D'Artagnan! We're a team! All for one and one for all . . ."

"You're not like them," his mother cautioned. "You're not of this time. All of them have grown up using swords. . . ."

"So have I."

"It's not the same," Dad said. "You studied fencing. And no matter how good you were, the fact is, when you lose a fencing match, you only lose points. When you lose a sword fight, you die."

Greg frowned. He knew his father was right, and in truth he was terrified of facing his enemies again. The only thing that scared him more, however, was being stranded in 1615 for the rest of his life.

"I know the Musketeers might not be the most formidable team in the world," Greg finally admitted. "But I also know that they need me. That's why the king made me one of them. Without my help, they'd never have been able to rescue you from La Mort. And without me I don't think they'll ever track down Dinicoeur—or the Devil's Stone."

In the dim light of the candle, Greg saw the color drain from his mother's face again. Even his father looked a bit shaken. He put an arm around Greg's mother, doing his best to comfort her.

Greg's mother turned to him, her eyes wet with tears. "Gregory, I don't want you putting your life at risk for us."

"Don't worry, Mom. The Musketeers and I will find Michel and Dominic—and the Devil's Stone. If all goes well, we won't be risking anything," Greg said, although he was quite sure that was a lie. Dinicoeur had lost the Devil's Stone once and it had cost him dearly. He wouldn't want to make that mistake twice. This time, Greg knew, when Dinicoeur found the stone, he would do everything in his power to protect it.

── FOUR

THE NEXT DAY, GREG AND THE OTHER MUSKETEERS woke at the crack of dawn to ride to the royal hunting grounds along with the king—and the king's staggeringly large entourage. There were four falconers, a squadron of soldiers, two dozen servants, and a coterie of distant relatives and other hangers-on. Despite all the attendants, King Louis was the only one allowed to participate in any of the actual falconry—although in truth, Louis really just sat on his horse and had other people do everything for him. The falconers brought him the birds. A stable boy held the reins of his horse. There were even servants armed with parasols to shade the king from the sun.

And for what? At the far end of the field, a gamekeeper would release a previously captured dove. Then, with great fanfare, Louis would remove the blindfold from his falcon, which would take off—and kill the dove.

That was it. To make it all worse, even if Greg had wanted to watch one bird kill another, the attack generally happened very far away, often quite high up in the sky, so that it merely looked like one dot flying into a slightly smaller dot.

While Greg found the whole process mind-numbing, everyone else seemed absolutely enthralled. Even Aramis, who Greg wouldn't have expected to root for the death of *anything*, was beside himself with excitement. "I never thought I'd ever get to see a real-live falcon hunt!" he confided to Greg. "Isn't it amazing?"

Amazingly dull, thought Greg, but he pasted on a smile for Aramis. "It sure is," he agreed, wondering what would happen if Aramis ever saw something that was actually exciting, like an action movie or the Super Bowl. The shock would probably kill him.

Greg shifted uncomfortably on his horse and took in his surroundings. The royal hunting grounds were merely a wide, open field of grass, bordered on three sides by farmland and on the fourth by woods. It *was* a pretty setting—Greg had to admit that—but it was also nasty hot out in the direct sun. Underneath his thick, woolen Musketeer outfit, Greg was sweating buckets.

Athos and Porthos were perched on their own horses close by. Athos seemed impervious to the heat, his back ramrod straight, looking like a soldier at all times. But Porthos made no secret of his discomfort as he slumped lazily in the saddle, his coat unbuttoned. "What say we make this interesting?" he called out, fanning a wad of money. "Anyone care to bet on the dove this time?"

Athos laughed but stopped suddenly, staring past Greg, his eyes narrowing. Greg turned in his saddle and found Milady de Winter approaching.

She rode a white horse and was dressed all in white to match. "Mind if I join you gentlemen?" she asked as she approached, fluttering a lace fan to keep from flushing in the heat.

"Not at all!" Aramis said, a bit too quickly. "It'd be our pleasure!"

Milady smiled and pulled her horse in between theirs, as close to Aramis as she could get. Greg glanced reflexively toward Athos, who failed to mask his jealousy.

Greg looked back at Milady and thought he caught *her* staring at Athos as well. As if, perhaps, she knew exactly what effect she was having on him—and was trying to provoke it.

It was the first time Greg had seen Milady since she'd whispered to him in the king's chambers the day before. "Good day, Milady," he said. "I was hoping to see you again.

I was wondering if we could discuss . . ."

"The falconry?" Milady said quickly. Before Greg could protest, she narrowed her eyes at him. "I'm surprised at how large a crowd has turned out," she said, waving a hand at all the attendants gathered close by. "One almost can't have a private thought out here."

Greg got the message: Keep his mouth shut for now. There were too many people around.

"What brings *you* here?" Athos asked sourly.

"The same thing as you, I'm sure," Milady replied. "The king requested my presence here. Until the queen arrives, I serve his will."

"Are you enjoying today's event?" Aramis asked.

"I'm afraid to say I find it a bit barbaric," Milady admitted. "But it's nice to be out of the city. On days like this, the smell really gets to me."

"Me, too," Greg said, before he could stop himself. It was true. The Seine reeked every day, as it was full of human waste. But in summer, the heat exacerbated the stench, which would then permeate the entire city.

"Yes, it is nice to be out here," Aramis put in. "Sometimes, you forget there's a whole world outside the city walls. And it's good for the king to see his subjects." He waved to the land around them.

In the surrounding fields, work had come to a standstill. Even though the king was probably just a distant, well-dressed dot to all the farmers, he was still the king.

It was possible that many of the subjects hadn't seen him for years, if ever. Most people simply stood in their fields, but a few had drawn closer and stood in the road, staring in awe at Louis, afraid to even set a toe on the royal hunting grounds for fear of being disrespectful. They were all farmers and their families, save for a group of dirt-streaked men tending an oxcart laden with massive white stones.

"Who are they?" Milady asked.

"Quarrymen," Aramis replied.

"And what's that they've got with them?" Milady wondered.

"Probably a future piece of the Louvre," Aramis said. "It's limestone. Almost anything of significance in the city is built of it—the bridges, the palace, the cathedrals . . . even Notre Dame. There must be a mine for it in those woods. You can hear the hammers."

Greg cocked his head and listened. Sure enough, from the direction of the woods he could hear the clink of metal against rock.

Milady heard it as well and turned to Aramis, impressed. "You're right, as usual. And I'm such a fool. I've lived in Paris my whole life and it's never once occurred to me to ask where all the stone came from!"

Greg frowned slightly. He was quite sure that Milady was no fool. In fact, he'd have bet that she knew exactly where the limestone came from and was merely buttering Aramis up.

A royal falconer approached Louis with yet another bird—an impressive beast, eighteen inches tall, with brown feathers and talons sharp enough to pierce metal. With its leather blindfold on, it sat so still it might have been carved from stone.

Aramis and Milady fell quiet out of respect. Everyone—even Porthos—sat up in their saddles, eyes riveted on the king, excited for another hunt.

Everyone except Greg. The excitement of watching a bird have its blindfold removed and take flight had died out fourteen flights before. Now he found his attention wandering to the far side of the field, near the woods, where the doves would be released. . . .

Something moved just beyond the tree line.

At first Greg thought his eyes were playing tricks on him, that it was merely a mirage caused by the heat rising off the field. But then he heard the distant twang of a taut string and the telltale whoosh of something slicing the air.

"Louis! Get down!" Greg yelled. He spurred his horse toward the king's.

Athos moved even faster. He'd recognized the sound of the incoming arrow in a fraction of a second—and in another fraction, he'd sprung from his horse to Louis's. He broadsided the king, and both boys tumbled to the ground while the falcon screeched and took flight. The arrow sailed past with a whoosh and embedded itself in the ground thirty feet beyond.

"What on earth . . . ?" Louis sputtered, aghast to have been knocked from his horse.

Athos was already on his feet, staring in the direction the arrow had come from. "Assassin!" he cried, springing back atop his steed. "Don't let him escape!"

His horse charged across the field. Greg and the other Musketeers spurred their horses as well and quickly fell in behind him. As they raced across the grass, Greg saw a figure duck back into the forest, a shadow moving quickly through the trees.

The Musketeers reached the woods, but the forest was too thick for the horses to pass through, so the boys quickly dismounted and followed on foot. They dashed through the trees, ducking branches and leaping roots in desperate pursuit of their quarry.

As they ran, however, Greg felt an idea nagging at him. Something was wrong, although everything had happened so quickly, he couldn't determine what it was. He replayed spotting the assassin, Athos's tackling the king, the flight of the arrow . . .

Up ahead, in the woods, the would-be killer paused and looked back at them before continuing on. It was a mere split second, but it struck Greg as odd, as though the assassin wanted to make sure they were following.

And suddenly, Greg knew.

He thought back to the arrow the assassin had fired. It had landed in the ground behind where Athos had been, not the king. Which meant it hadn't been meant for the king at all.

It had been meant for Athos.

"Athos! Stop!" Greg cried. "It's a trap!"

The urgency in his voice froze the others in their tracks. They spun toward him, understanding on Aramis's face, confusion on the others'.

And then the attack came.

FIVE

THERE WERE FOUR OF THEM, ARMED WITH BOWS AND arrows, shrouded in black. Greg spun on his heel and changed direction before they could fire. The other Musketeers, alerted by his warning, did the same—although there was no time to coordinate. Everyone went a different direction at once.

The bows twanged and the arrows screamed through the air. Greg heard one whistle past his head and thunk into a tree. Then the attackers shouted in a language he didn't understand and gave chase.

Greg could hear one of the assassins coming through the woods behind him, but he didn't dare look back. He ran with all his might, fighting his way through the underbrush, not knowing where he was going, simply moving as fast as he could.

And suddenly he caught a glimpse of someone off to the side, watching from the cover of the trees. A burly, muscular man with a thick mustache and hatred in his eyes.

René Valois.

Greg risked another glance in that direction, but Valois had vanished. Still, Greg was sure it had been Dinicoeur's henchman. He veered in the opposite direction, not wanting to go anywhere near Valois. Ahead, the woods brightened. Greg crashed through the underbrush and found himself in a large, man-made clearing. Three grimy, muscled men gaped at him as he burst from the trees, waving and yelling, *"Arrêtez!"* Stop!

At first, Greg thought they were yelling at his pursuer, telling him to back off and leave the poor kid he was chasing alone. But then Greg realized they were telling *him* to stop, pointing at something hidden in the tall grass. But it was too late; he was already right on top of it. . . .

The limestone mine—a big, gaping hole, plunging deep into the earth. It was four feet across with a ladder jutting out of it. Greg skidded to a stop, teetered on the brink— and then toppled over the edge.

Darkness swallowed him. He lashed out as he fell,

grabbing for anything he could. His right hand caught something and he held tight, jerking to a stop so hard he thought his arm might rip loose from the socket. His sword slipped from its sheath and plunged into the shaft, clattering on the ground below.

Greg had caught a rung of the miners' ladder, and it splintered and cracked from his sudden weight. Going down was dark and quite likely a dead end, but he was already so far from the top, there was no other choice. He quickly scrambled down the ladder, even though his shoulder was screaming with pain.

A shadow suddenly blotted out what little light there was above. The assassin was coming after him, grabbing the ladder and sliding down quickly, faster than Greg could climb.

Greg had no choice but to jump and pray the bottom of the shaft wasn't too far below. There was a sickening moment as he hung in the air—but then his feet slammed into the ground and he tumbled. He caught a glimpse of his sword, illuminated by the single shaft of sunlight, and snatched it up just before the assassin thudded to earth.

The man was huge, well over a foot taller than Greg. Instead of a mere rapier, he carried a scimitar big enough to slice Greg's head off with one shot. Greg knew there was no way he could beat the guy in a fight.

So he ran, plunging deeper into the darkness. The mine tunnels forked again and again; Greg ducked one way, then the other. The vinegar-like scent of limestone made his eyes water, but he kept on going, hoping he could lose his pursuer. Unfortunately, his footsteps echoed loudly in the otherwise silent passage, giving away the path he'd chosen every time. He knew he had to try something different.

After rounding a corner, Greg stopped running and flattened himself against the wall. The moment his pursuer came flying around the turn, Greg bolted back the way he'd come. The assassin was so big he couldn't change direction quite as quickly as Greg, but he still was faster than Greg had anticipated. As Greg charged back through the mine, he could hear the big man thundering behind him, only a few yards back. His strength didn't seem to be flagging at all, while Greg felt like he was cruising on fumes.

Ahead, Greg saw a shaft of light beaming down into the mine again, so bright after his time in the darkness that it was almost blinding. It wasn't until he stumbled toward it that he discovered it wasn't the same shaft he'd come down; he'd gotten turned around in the mine somehow. This one was much larger, ten feet across, designed for taking the huge chunks of limestone out through it. A wooden pallet of stone was currently being winched up toward the opening above.

Another rickety ladder extended toward the surface. Greg scrambled up it, knowing he had to move fast if he hoped to escape through the opening before the pallet blocked it. But his energy was almost spent; it took every last drop of adrenaline he had to climb.

He'd just skirted past the pallet and was nearly to the top when the ladder trembled violently. In one terrifying instant, Greg realized he'd made a mistake. The man below didn't *have* to climb up after him; he could catch Greg by simply taking out the ladder. Greg lunged for the lip of earth above him just as the ladder collapsed below. He caught the grassy edge with his fingertips and clung there for a moment. He had a glimpse of the intricate block and tackle system arranged over the hole—and then his fingers slipped from the edge and he dropped back into the mine.

He tumbled backward through the air, but the fall wasn't nearly as far as he expected. He quickly slammed into stone, and it took him a second to realize he'd landed on the pallet, not the ground below. However, his sudden weight on the pallet overwhelmed the block and tackle that supported it. Above him, a pulley ripped free of the support beam and the rope went slack. Greg dropped again, only this time he was riding the pallet. Halfway down, the rope caught again as the other pulleys held, and the entire pallet jerked to a stop with such force that it broke apart. Greg clung to the rope as the pallet disintegrated beneath him, scattering its load of stone.

Below, Greg heard a terrified scream, followed by a sickening wet crunch. When he finally gathered the nerve to look down, he saw the assassin at the base of the shaft, squashed beneath a massive block of limestone.

Greg's stomach churned, and he quickly looked away.

"*Sacre bleu!*" Porthos's voice echoed through the mineshaft. Greg looked up to see his fellow Musketeer perched on the rim above. "Now that's what I call knocking your enemy flat!"

Greg was surprised his friend could joke at a time like this, but Porthos's humor tempered the shock of having been involved in the death of another person, however deserving.

"Hold on tight," Porthos told him. "We'll get you out of there soon."

A few seconds later, the rope began to rise, pulling Greg up with it. Soon he emerged into daylight to see an ox team tugging the other end of the rope. Greg collapsed in the grass, exhausted.

Athos was close by, talking to a group of miners. Aramis was there, too, looking far more shaken from the battle than the others. He approached the edge of the pit, looked down at what remained of Greg's attacker and recoiled, green with nausea.

"What happened up here?" Greg asked, to distract him.

"We ran the others off," Aramis reported.

An image suddenly returned to Greg from his dash through the woods: the man with the mustache and hatred in his eyes. "Valois was with them," he said.

The others all turned to him, surprised. "You saw him?" Porthos asked.

Greg nodded. "Only for a second, but I'm sure it was him. He must have been in command of the assassins. Why else would he have been here?"

"How'd he link up with a team of assassins?" Aramis asked. "And foreign assassins at that?"

"How could you tell they were foreigners?" Porthos asked.

"Because they weren't speaking French," Aramis replied. Porthos nodded understanding. "Then who were they?"

"We'll know soon enough." Athos came over, leading two miners with another ladder slung between them. He pointed to the shaft, and the men dutifully lowered the ladder into it.

Aramis turned even greener. "Oh no. You can't possibly expect us all to go down there and see the . . . ah . . . remains."

"Don't worry," Athos said. "You two stay here and rest. Porthos and I can handle it."

"We can?" Porthos asked, going pale.

"Unless you'd prefer all the queen's handmaidens to know you were afraid of a dead body." Athos grinned, then descended gamely into the pit.

"It's not a dead body. It's a *squashed* body," Porthos muttered, but Athos's goad had worked, and he clambered down the ladder himself.

While they waited, Aramis filled Greg in on the details of how the others had fended off the assassins, who had ultimately fled on horseback. Pursuing them had been out of the question, however—the boys' horses were too far away to recover in time—and besides, they were all concerned for Greg's well-being. Aramis admitted they'd all been mighty relieved to find Greg alive; the odds had seemed much more likely that *he'd* have been the body left in the pit, rather than the other way around.

Finally, they heard the ladder creaking and groaning until Porthos and Athos emerged over the edge.

"Well?" Greg asked expectantly. "Any idea who he is?"

"Since he's dead, he didn't respond very well to questioning," Porthos said. "But he was wearing *this*." He handed Greg a swatch of the man's clothing.

Now, in broad daylight, while he wasn't running for his life, Greg had his first chance to take a good look at it. He and Aramis had the same thought at once.

"It's silk," Aramis said. He examined the fabric closely. "Just like the piece we found from Milady's mysterious man at the inn."

"He also had *this* on him." Athos held out a piece of parchment.

Aramis took it, trying to ignore the blood spattered on it. It was folded over three times and had been sealed with red wax, although the seal had been shattered so that only a wedge of it remained. It would have been the top of the seal, displaying a small crown sandwiched between what Greg thought might have been a P and an R.

Aramis unfolded the parchment and frowned. "I'm not familiar with this language," he said with a sigh.

Greg glanced at the letter over Aramis's shoulder. The text was written in a florid, ornate script, but he could make out the words: *El portador de esta carta es un emisario del rey de España. . . .* "It's Spanish," he said.

Athos and Porthos looked at him, surprised—which they always did when he, rather than Aramis, turned out to actually know something. And then understanding dawned on Athos. "Of course you know that! You're from Artagnan, and it's right by Spain."

"Right." Greg tried to sound convincing.

"What does it say?" Porthos asked.

"I can't actually read it. But it's something like 'he who carries this letter . . .'"

"It's an emissary note!" Aramis said. When Greg looked at him blankly, he explained. "They're written for people traveling in foreign lands on official business. So they can properly present themselves." He looked back at the wax seal fragment with renewed understanding. "This man was an emissary of the king of Spain."

The other three boys gasped. "How do you know?" Athos asked.

Aramis pointed to the crown at the top of the seal. "That's the sign of a king. The 'P' is for 'Philip,' king of Spain. And the 'R' is for 'Rex,' or 'king' in Latin."

"So," Athos said, "two months ago Dinicoeur had Milady

deliver a letter to a man in Spanish silks. And today Dini-coeur's right-hand man, Valois, seemingly oversees four men sent by King Philip to kill us. You realize what this means?"

Aramis nodded. "Dinicoeur and Richelieu are in league with Spain."

The other Musketeers frowned, aware how serious this was. "We'd better tell the king," Greg said.

SIX

Louis XIII sat on his throne, listening intently to every word the Musketeers said. Once they were done relating the events of the day, his brow furrowed with concern. "Obviously Valois is connected to these Spanish assassins," he said. "But are you sure that links Dinicoeur and Richelieu to them? Is there any chance Valois could have been acting on his own?"

"I'd doubt that, Your Majesty," Athos replied, shaking his head. "I know Valois well, as I served under him as a member of the King's Guard. He is very good at carrying out orders, but he is a follower, not a leader."

"And we know he's following Dinicoeur, rather than one of my other enemies? I've heard rumors that the Prince of Condé is plotting against me."

Aramis stepped forward. "The last time Valois was seen, he was aiding Dinicoeur and Richelieu in Richelieu's escape from the Bastille. It's obvious that he has thrown his lot in with them. Given his involvement today, we're assuming that Dinicoeur has made some sort of alliance with Spain, then sent the assassins back here to take care of us under Valois' command."

"But why go after the four of you, rather than me?" Louis asked. "And what would this alliance be, exactly? Dinicoeur has been expelled from my court. What could he possibly have to offer Spain?"

"We don't know," Aramis admitted.

"Then we must find out at once." The king looked over at the Musketeers. "How soon can the four of you be prepared to leave?"

Greg was completely caught off guard—and he noticed Aramis and Porthos reacting with surprise as well. Only Athos seemed pleased by the question. "Within the hour," he replied, his eyes, glittering with excitement.

"Hold on a moment," Porthos said. "You want *us* to go to Spain?"

"I want you to track down Richelieu and Dinicoeur," Louis replied. "If the trail leads to Spain, so be it."

"Why us?" Aramis asked. "Surely there are members of the King's Guard more qualified for such an arduous journey. . . ."

"I do not question your qualifications," said Louis. "You have proven your mettle before. That is why I chose to make you Musketeers. Your job is to protect the throne—and I cannot imagine a bigger threat to the throne right now than Spain rising against us. It would mean that my upcoming marriage is merely a ruse to lull us into complacency."

"Wait," Greg said. "How could the marriage be a *Spanish* ruse? I thought you were marrying Anne of Austria."

Everyone in the room turned to Greg. "Where, exactly, do you think Anne of Austria is from?" Louis asked.

"Um . . . Austria?" Greg ventured.

Athos and Porthos both rolled their eyes. "No," Aramis said. "She's the daughter of Philip, the king of Spain."

"Then why is she called 'Anne of Austria'?" Greg demanded.

"Because her *mother's* from Austria," Aramis explained, as though it was obvious.

"That still doesn't make sense," Greg said defensively. "If she's from Spain, she should be called Anne of Spain—"

"Anne's name isn't important right now," Louis said sharply. "What *is* important are the motives of Anne's father, King Phillip. He has claimed this marriage is to broker a peace between France and the Habsburg Empire, but I have long suspected that he would prefer to control our country outright."

"Why is that?" Aramis asked.

"Have any of you ever heard of the Spanish Road?" Louis asked.

Greg, Porthos, and Athos shook their heads. To their surprise, Aramis did, too.

"I'd have suspected not." Louis sighed. "It doesn't go through France—yet. You see, Spain, on our southern border, rules the Habsburg Netherlands, on our northeast. Spain has to provide the Netherlands with troops and supplies, but we have never given them permission to pass through our country, so instead the Spanish have to go by boat from Barcelona to Milan, then over the Alps all the way across Europe. *That's* the Spanish Road. It's an extremely treacherous route that can take over a year. It would be far preferable for them to pass through France, for which reason Anne has been betrothed to me. . . ."

"I'm sorry," Greg said, aghast. "Philip agreed to marry his daughter off just to get a more direct route to the Netherlands?"

Everyone swiveled to stare at him once again. Greg realized, a little too late, that he'd just let his modern-day sensibilities show.

"Every royal marriage brokers some peace or another," the king explained. "It's the way of the world. But suppose that Philip never intended to marry Anne off at all? Or perhaps, he *was* willing to do it—and then Dinicoeur came to him with a better offer. If either of those scenarios is true, then this marriage is a sham designed to distract us."

"From what?" Athos asked.

"That's what you need to find out," the king said. "You shall leave as soon as possible. Dinicoeur and Richelieu were last seen fleeing south, most likely headed toward the Rhône River. I understand that's the fastest way to Spain. You should head that way yourselves. Take the Rhône south to the city of Arles, then cross southern France overland to the Pyrenees Mountains. Whatever you learn, send messages back via homing pigeon. Hopefully, you'll figure out Dinicoeur's plans before you reach Spain itself, but if you must, proceed into that country with caution."

Greg looked at Louis, impressed. Louis was sounding like a proper king, so different from the boy he had met with days before.

"You don't have to worry about us." Athos whipped out his sword and slashed the air. "We can handle ourselves."

Louis raised a hand, signaling Athos to sheath his blade. "I'd prefer this was a *diplomatic* mission. I need you to make as few waves as possible. Our peace with Spain is delicate enough as it is. You must proceed with great caution."

"Wow," Porthos muttered under his breath. "This sounds better and better all the time."

Aramis stepped forward, looking a bit pale. "Not to question your judgment, Your Highness, but this is a very long journey. And none of us have ever been out of sight of Paris. . . ."

"Save for D'Artagnan." Louis nodded toward Greg, who felt his heart sink. "His hometown is close to the Spanish border. He got here. Thus, he must have some knowledge of the open road."

Greg's concern about the trip suddenly grew a hundred times worse. "To be honest," he said, "I didn't exactly come to Paris over the Rhône. . . ."

"Even better!" the king exclaimed. "Then you know another route back to Paris, should there be trouble."

"Ah, well, the thing is . . . I'm not exactly comfortable with the fate of our excursion resting on my knowledge of France," Greg stammered. "I don't know if it's entirely reliable. . . ."

"On the contrary," Louis said. "You four are as reliable as they come. The truth is, you are the only ones I *know* I can trust. I know I'm asking a great deal of you, but you have served me valiantly in the past, and I expect that you can do it once again."

Athos knelt before Louis and bowed his head. "It is my honor to serve the crown on this mission," he said.

To either side of Greg, Aramis and Porthos knelt as well, though a bit more reluctantly. Despite his serious misgivings about the mission, Greg saw no choice but to join the crowd. "It is my honor as well," he said, kneeling.

Louis beamed at them proudly. "No, the honor is

mine—to have as impressive a team as this. Now depart, before any more time slips away."

The Musketeers stood again, and Louis dismissed them with a casual wave. They obediently turned and left the throne room.

In the hall, Aramis wasted no time in giving them all assignments. "Athos, take care of the horses and weapons. We'll need four extra steeds to carry our gear. Porthos, you're in charge of provisions and water. I'll go to the royal cote and the homing pigeons. D'Artagnan, you've traveled the farthest among us. Get whatever supplies you think are necessary for the long journey. I'd like to leave before the hour is up so we can get some distance before the sun sets."

The others nodded agreement and quickly scattered, leaving Greg alone in the palace. He immediately sagged against the wall, overwhelmed. He'd had a hard enough time getting by in medieval Paris; how was he going to survive a grueling trip into hostile territory? He didn't have the traveling expertise Louis thought he did—which meant he might be endangering the mission, rather than helping it.

The mere thought of leaving made his legs tremble. What he really needed to do was head back into the throne room and tell the king he was making a big mistake. Greg would be able to serve Louis far better here. . . .

"Gregory."

Greg leaped, startled, but then recognized the voice. He turned to find his father coming up next to him.

"Sorry! Didn't mean to frighten you." Dad looked at him curiously. "What's wrong?"

Greg looked up at his dad and sighed. "Well," he started, then recounted the new task he and the Musketeers had been given.

Greg's father shook his head. "That's it. I'm coming with you," he said.

Greg felt a surge of respect for his father but shook his head. "You can't, Dad. You need to stay here and take care of Mom. She needs you. I'll have the other Musketeers to look out for me." Greg didn't mention the other reason he felt his father should stay: Dad was hopeless in the outdoors.

Now Dad smiled weakly at him but nodded in defeat. "I suppose you're right. I just wish I could do more to help. . . ."

"You *can*. Keep a watch on the palace, and"—he lowered his voice—"Aramis found something about the Devil's Stone being connected to a place called the White City of Emperor Constantine. Do you know what that could be?"

Dad blinked, looking thrown. "No."

"Well, we need to find out. Aramis won't be able to research it any more. He's been going through the archives at Notre Dame. Maybe you could continue his work."

"I suppose I could, but . . ."

"Hopefully, it won't even be necessary. If we can track down Dinicoeur, there's a good chance he'll lead me right to the Devil's Stone. And once I have it, we will be able to get home and all our problems will be over."

To Greg's surprise, his father shook his head. "Greg, we have much bigger problems than getting home."

"What do you mean?"

"Well, finding the stone and returning back to our own time is important, of course. At least, it is to *us*. But what's happening is much bigger than us. If Michel Dinicoeur is actually plotting with the Spanish against France, then he's hoping to alter all of human history. In the future we came from, Louis married Anne of Austria. Their son, Louis the Fourteenth, became one of the great kings of France. If Dominic prevents even that single event from happening—let alone does something colossal like helping Spain overthrow France—who knows what the ripple effects will be?"

Greg stopped and looked at his father. "You mean . . . even if we returned to our own time, it wouldn't be the time we knew anymore?"

"Exactly," Dad said gravely. "This mission is of far greater importance than anyone here can possibly imagine. The fate of the entire world is at stake."

Greg swallowed. His mission had seemed daunting before when he'd thought only his own life was at risk. Now it was completely overwhelming. And yet he knew he couldn't back out. He pasted on a smile he hoped looked reassuring. "Don't worry about me," he said. "I'm off to Spain—and I'll be back with the Devil's Stone."

PART TWO

THE CHASE

SEVEN

Madrid

THE SOLDIER STATIONED AT THE FRONT GATE OF THE ALCÁ-zar went on alert as Michel Dinicoeur approached. This was understandable, as it was three o'clock in the morning. "Stop," he said, raising a hand. "What is your business?"

"I am here to see King Philip," Michel replied.

"At this time of night?" the soldier asked, incredulous. "The king is asleep."

"That's fine," Michel told him. "I only want to *see* the fool. Not talk to him."

With that, he leaped at the soldier.

The man was considerably bigger than Michel, and even though Michel was in extremely good shape for a four-hundred-year-old man, he knew there was no chance he could win a fair fight. But then, Michel had no intention of fighting fair. He had chloroform.

The anesthetic wouldn't be discovered officially for another two hundred and fifty years, but it wasn't too hard to get if you knew how. It was produced naturally by certain types of seaweed—and a little went a long way. The small bit he'd dabbed on the rag in his hand was more than enough to render the other man unconscious.

It wasn't instantaneous, though. Even after Michel had leaped onto the soldier's back and pressed the rag to his mouth, the big man clawed at him. But a few seconds later, he collapsed in a heap, and Michel dragged him into the shadows and slipped into the castle.

There were other soldiers to confront on the way to the king's quarters, but far less than there would have been during the day. Michel had studied the castle carefully over the past week, watching the soldiers on their nighttime patrols, determining the best time to attack. Now the castle guards were few and far between. Several had fallen asleep at their posts and were easy to dispatch. Others gave him considerably more trouble. One actually scored a hit with his blade that might have killed a mortal man, but then he'd let his guard down, expecting Michel to die—and Michel had quickly taken him out.

Within fifteen minutes of entering the castle, Michel had reached the king's bedroom, not far from the throne room. The door wasn't even locked—what was the point of locking a door when you had an entire army to protect you? It creaked as Michel opened it, but Philip remained sound asleep.

A single candle illuminated the room, burning low after being lit all night. Michel shut the door behind him and approached the small bed.

In the gleam of the candlelight, Michel could see the silver links of the chain that bore the half of the Devil's Stone around Philip's neck. He stepped forward with the chloroform-soaked rag.

Philip's eyes suddenly snapped open. When he saw Michel, he reacted with confusion, rather than fear—as though unsure whether he was dreaming or not. "How . . . ?" he gasped. "How are you here? You should be in France by now."

"I am," Michel replied, then placed the rag to Philip's lips.

The king put up far less of a fight than any of his guards had. He was a much weaker man, and his screams for help were muffled by the rag. Within seconds, he was limp.

His hands trembling with anticipation, Michel pulled the silver chain off Philip's neck. The piece of the Devil's Stone gleamed darkly as he lifted it into the candlelight.

Michel felt a flow of warmth surge through him as he

laid the chain around his own neck. It had been nearly four hundred years since he'd last held this piece of the stone—save for an all-too-brief few minutes in the Louvre two months earlier, before Greg and his parents had ruined everything. But now it was as if no time had passed at all. He needed both halves of the stone to make Dominic immortal, but this piece alone still had power. It made him feel strong again, like he could do anything.

Michel took a dagger from its sheath and placed it at the king's neck. No point in leaving any loose ends.

Before he could do anything, however, he heard footsteps racing toward the bedroom. Soldiers yelled in Spanish: "We have been invaded!" "Get to the king!" "Make sure he's safe!"

Michel quickly withdrew the dagger and darted from the room. There was another way out through Philip's private quarters, and as he ducked through the door, he heard the guards burst into the king's bedroom, then cry with fear when Philip didn't wake. The anesthetized king distracted them while Michel slunk through the castle. He kept to the shadows, and soon he was back out on the streets of Madrid, the half of the Devil's Stone clutched to his chest.

He felt fantastic with it. Immortal. The wound where the soldier had stabbed him before barely hurt anymore. It was already healing quickly, thanks to the stone's power.

But as good as the stone made him feel, he knew he would have to give it up soon. Once Dominic was immortal—and the Musketeers were dead—Dominic would have the life Michel had longed for: an eternal life of wealth and power. In making that happen—in altering Dominic's course— Michel would then change his own. There would be no need for Michel to return through time. In essence, the person he was now might even vanish from existence, but he didn't care. His life had been miserable, thanks to the Musketeers.

Michel paused for a moment, thinking about them— and that meddlesome Greg Rich. If all had gone well, Valois and the assassins should have taken care of them by now. Michel had assumed he'd know when the boys were dead—as though their deaths might somehow send a ripple through the space-time continuum that he could feel. Now he began to wonder if something had gone wrong.

Michel quickened his pace through the dark streets. Perhaps it didn't matter whether the Musketeers lived or not. He had half the Devil's Stone. He had to get to Dominic, who *was* in France. Then they would recover the second half of the Devil's Stone—and Michel's work here would be done.

His horse was tethered close to the Alcázar. Even though it was the middle of the night, there was no time to lose. The king's soldiers would soon be searching the city for him. He climbed astride his steed and rode north, toward France.

EIGHT

The forest seemed to go on forever.

The Musketeers had been traveling for four days now, and they'd seen almost nothing but trees.

The other boys weren't surprised by this, but Greg found it astonishing. The world had changed far more than he could have possibly imagined over four hundred years. Back in modern times, he'd stared at this land from the window of a plane on approach to Paris. There had barely been any forest at all. The entire swath from Paris to the Rhône River had been a giant patchwork of tilled fields dotted with hundreds of towns and crisscrossed by a thousand roads.

But now, in the past, it was all forest—thick, dark, primordial forest. Many of the trees were staggeringly large, with trunks as big as houses and branches that soared high above and blotted out the sun. The underbrush was an impenetrable tangle of bushes and vines. There was only one route through it, a thin path that meandered between the huge trees.

"This isn't what I thought it'd be," Athos confided to the others on the fourth day. They were riding their horses single file along the narrow path. Even in the middle of the day, the woods were so dark it seemed like twilight.

"And what *did* you expect?" Aramis asked.

"I don't know, exactly. I'd heard the woods went on a long ways, I just didn't think it'd be *this* long." Athos gave Aramis an accusing look. "Perhaps we made a wrong turn somewhere."

"We didn't," Aramis said curtly.

"You don't know that for sure," Athos argued. "We might all be riding in circles."

"If we were riding in circles, the sun would be moving around us," Aramis told him. "But it's not. It's rising on our left and setting on our right. Therefore, we're heading south, which is the correct direction."

Athos considered this a moment, then shook his head. "That can't be right. These woods are too big. We must have made a mistake."

"We didn't!" Aramis snapped. "Athos, I know what I'm doing. The world is simply much larger than your tiny brain can comprehend."

Porthos laughed. Athos recoiled, offended, although he didn't say anything in response. Instead, he glowered at the others, angry with Aramis for the insult—and with Porthos for laughing at it.

Greg turned away, doing his best to hide his concern. He'd expected the journey to be long and dangerous, but something had arisen lately that worried him even more: His fellow Musketeers weren't getting along.

Greg had assumed that the one good thing about this trip would be the camaraderie. He'd imagined Porthos regaling them with funny stories, Athos relating his adventures in the King's Guard, Aramis pointing out the constellations around the campfire every night. Instead, Athos and Aramis had been at each other's throats since the first day, while Porthos had spent most of the time complaining. They simply weren't working as a team.

"D'Artagnan, you're the best traveled of us all," Athos said, unwilling to let his disagreement with Aramis drop. "Is it truly possible that these woods could be this large? Or are we going in circles?"

Greg winced. "Well, like I've said, I haven't been through *these* woods before. . . ."

"Yes, we know." Aramis looked at Greg expectantly. "But you have traveled great distances and know how big France is, correct? So answer Athos. Who is right?"

Greg looked to Porthos for help, but his fellow Mus-keteer deliberately avoided his gaze, staring off into the woods.

Greg reluctantly turned back to Aramis. "You're right," he said.

Athos shot him a wounded look, as though Greg had betrayed him.

"It's the truth," Greg tried to explain. "France is a very big country. It could take us several *weeks* to get to Spain on horseback."

"What?" Porthos asked, suddenly jolted into the conver-sation. "Several weeks just to get there?"

"I told the king this would be a very long journey," Aramis chided. "Exactly what did you think that meant?"

Porthos lowered his eyes, embarrassed. "A week or two."

"We'll be lucky if we make it to Arles in a week or two!" Aramis said. "We don't merely have to get to Spain. We have to track down Michel and Dominic and find out what they're up to. After which we'll have to get all the way back to Paris. How on earth did you think this would only take fourteen days?"

"Math isn't exactly my strong suit," Porthos admitted.

"*Thinking* isn't your strong suit," Athos muttered. "What do you think we packed all this gear for?" He waved a hand at the four horses behind them, heavily laden with food and supplies.

Porthos shrugged. "I thought we were just being over-prepared."

The horses carried food and water, which the boys were supplementing by hunting and gathering. There were also some coarse blankets to sleep on and fashion crude shelters from, weapons ranging from crossbows to broadswords, emissary notes, a small bit of silver to purchase additional supplies, and a cage with five homing pigeons to send messages of their progress back to the king. That was the extent of their supplies. They didn't even have so much as an extra set of clothes. After four days in the heat, everyone's uniform already stank of sweat and horse.

"Porthos," Greg said, "I don't want to alarm you, but it might be *months* until we return to Paris."

Porthos gasped in horror. "Months? Maybe this mission wasn't such a good idea. I have things to do back in Paris, you know. Family matters. Dances I have agreed to attend. Women to woo . . ."

"I'm sure we'd *all* like to be back in Paris, but we have things we *must* do in Spain." Aramis spoke with surprising confidence. "The king himself chose us to find out what Michel and Dominic are plotting. If we turn our back on our responsibilities, who knows what trouble they will wreak?"

"Yes, but one of our responsibilities is to protect the king," Porthos said. "So perhaps one of us should go back. Just to make sure he's safe."

"If you don't want to continue with us, you're welcome to go." Athos pointed behind them at the path through the dark woods. "It's only four days back through this forest. *Alone*."

Porthos swallowed. It was obvious he hadn't thought that part through as well. "On second thought, maybe I'll stay with all of you."

"I suspected as much." Athos snapped his reins and rode on. The others obediently followed.

Porthos pulled up alongside Greg a few minutes later and confided, "I don't know if I can do this. This trip was daunting enough when I thought it would only take a fortnight. But now . . ." He glanced around the forest warily. "I hate these woods. I'd rather face Michel and Dominic than spend another day in them."

"Why's that?" Greg asked. He was dreading the moment when he'd have to confront Michel and Dominic again.

"Because the woods are dangerous!" Porthos said emphatically. "They're crawling with thieves, bandits, and vagabonds who'll happily slit our throats in return for all our gear."

Athos laughed mockingly. "Don't worry yourself about that. No band of thieves stands a chance against me."

"While you're awake, maybe," Porthos shot back. "But you have to sleep sometime. And that's when they get you. They lurk in the woods, waiting for the chance to kill you."

"The stories about the woods being full of thieves are

merely rumors," Aramis chided. "They're not true."

"Really?" Greg asked, feeling better to hear this.

"Really," Aramis said. "What we *need* to worry about are the wolves."

"Wolves?" Greg suddenly felt worried again.

"Yes. They surround men, hunting as a team, and pick off people one by one, ripping open their gullets and feasting on their entrails."

Porthos gulped. "Thank you, Aramis. I was only worried before. But now I'm downright terrified."

Aramis shrugged. "Ignorance of the truth is a recipe for disaster."

"I'm not worried about any wolves." Athos unsheathed his sword and slashed at imaginary beasts. "They are only flesh and blood. I can handle them. We have nothing to fear on this journey."

"What about the assassins?" The words just slipped out of Greg's mouth. He couldn't control it; the assassins had been weighing on his mind for days.

He could tell from the looks in the others' eyes that the same held true for them. Even Athos seemed concerned, though he tried to cover it with his usual bravado. "We took care of them last time. I think they've learned not to mess with us."

"We got *lucky* last time," Aramis countered. "If D'Artagnan hadn't realized they were about to ambush us, we'd all be dead. They know that. They're not going to give up because they failed to kill us once. Especially not with Valois commanding them."

Porthos and Greg nodded agreement, though Athos remained unswayed.

"If they're targeting us, where are they, then?" the swordsman asked. "I haven't seen hide nor hair of them over the last four days."

"You're not supposed to see hide nor hair of them," Porthos muttered. "That's what makes them assassins."

"I don't know," Aramis told Athos. "Perhaps we left Paris so quickly, they didn't notice. But if that's the case, it won't take Valois long to figure out that we've gone—and where we're going. Or maybe they're well aware of what we're doing and are just waiting for the right moment to attack."

"Are we all *sure* we shouldn't just turn around and go home again?" Porthos asked weakly.

"We can't turn back," Greg said as the others shook their heads. "This mission is far too important." He caught Aramis's gaze as he said it. Of all the Musketeers, Aramis was the only one who knew enough about Dinicoeur and the Devil's Stone to fully comprehend how much was at stake.

"D'Artagnan's right," Aramis agreed. "We swore to protect the king and France, and that is what we must do now, no matter how daunting. We have a duty to learn what Dinicoeur is up to and send word of it back to the king."

"And what if it's not that simple?" Porthos asked. "What happens if we go all this way, and finally track down

Dinicoeur and Richelieu—and find that their plans are already well under way? What if there's no time for us to send a pigeon back to Paris and wait for reinforcements to arrive? What are we supposed to do then?"

Greg grimaced. This thought had occurred to him plenty of times along the way. Now he could see in the others' faces that the same concern had plagued them as well.

"I pray that such a situation will not arise," Aramis said finally. "But should it, I have faith in our abilities. We rescued Greg's parents from a prison everyone believed was impenetrable—and defeated our enemies to boot."

"That doesn't mean we can handle *anything* that comes our way," Porthos shot back. "What if—"

Athos suddenly raised a hand and signaled him to be quiet.

Greg listened to the woods, which were surprisingly silent. Save for the faint chirr of an insect now and then, there was virtually no noise. It was so quiet, Greg could hear his own heart beating in his chest.

And there, faintly in the distance, came the sound of hoofbeats.

"Three horses," Athos said. "Coming quickly. Take cover."

The boys quickly guided the horses off the narrow trail and into the darkness of the woods. Greg found himself gripped by fear.

Athos took the point, watching the trail through a gap in the trees. Greg and the other boys were too far back in the thick underbrush to see anything.

The thundering of hooves grew closer and closer, then suddenly stopped. Greg listened as hard as he could; he thought he could pick out the faint sound of the horses now proceeding slowly, trying to be as quiet as possible. Their pursuers must have realized something was wrong.

Athos tensed in his saddle and tightened his grip on his blade.

The sound of the approaching horses came closer and closer. Through a gap in the underbrush, Greg saw the other party emerge from behind a tree. There were two riders, both shrouded in heavy cloaks; one had a thin sword in hand, the other a loaded crossbow. The third horse was being used to haul gear.

The riders suddenly went rigid, as though they had sensed the Musketeers' presence. They spun toward the place where the boys were hidden, raising their weapons.

But Athos had already sprung into action. His horse charged onto the road, and as it did, Athos leaped from the saddle. He knocked the first rider's sword away as he flew through the air and slammed into the second. Both Musketeer and rider tumbled off the horse. The crossbow discharged. The bolt whistled above Greg's head and embedded itself harmlessly in a tree.

Athos and the rider crashed to the ground in a heap. The

rider yelped in pain, then snapped, "Athos! Get off of me, you idiot!"

Greg gasped, recognizing the voice.

Athos scrambled away from his opponent, equally surprised.

The rider stood and pulled back her cowl, revealing her face.

Milady de Winter.

✦ NINE

THE RIDER ACCOMPANYING MILADY DE WINTER WAS ALSO a girl. Her name was Catherine and she was thirteen, though like everyone else Greg had met in 1615, she seemed older. Catherine was in training to be a handmaiden to the future queen, and thus answered to Milady. She said little, allowing Milady to do most of the talking, although Greg perceived a great intelligence in her eyes; Milady wouldn't have brought just *any* girl along with her on such a treacherous journey. And while Catherine wasn't as blatantly gorgeous as Milady, who drew the eye of every man when she walked into a room, she was beautiful nonetheless. Hers was simply a more subtle beauty. Greg hadn't really noticed her at first, but now, as everyone sat around a roaring campfire, Greg found himself stealing glances at Catherine whenever he could.

The sun had set and they were all eating dinner, rabbits that Athos and Porthos had killed, skinned, and set on spits over the flames. Two months before, Greg would have found the idea of eating a rabbit nauseating. Now, famished after a long day on the road, he devoured his portion within minutes. The girls were even hungrier. They made a faint attempt at decorum when the food was served, then dug in ravenously.

Porthos found this hilarious. "Whoa there!" he laughed. "Slow down, ladies. The food's not going to hop away."

Catherine reddened, embarrassed, but Milady just said, "We haven't had much time to eat over the last three days. We were trying to go as fast as possible to catch up to you. We figured you'd be trying to make good time yourselves."

"So . . . you left the day after us, then?" Greg asked.

"Yes," Milady said.

"Why didn't you just come with us?" Aramis asked.

"Well, no one said you were leaving—or where you were going," Milady replied. "You all simply disappeared, almost no one knew where or why, and those few who did were determined to keep it a secret."

"How'd you find out, then?" Porthos asked.

"How do you think?" Milady batted her eyes at him, showing off just the tiniest bit of the power her beauty had. "Most men are weak. They'll tell you anything you need in return for a smile."

"Not me, sister," Porthos said. "You want to learn anything from me, it'll cost you at least a kiss."

Milady laughed—although Greg noticed that Athos and Aramis both looked annoyed at Porthos's flirtation. Greg had hoped that the girls' presence in camp might temper the antagonism between Athos and Aramis, but sadly, it had made things even worse. Both were constantly vying for Milady's attention—and annoyed by any favoritism she showed the other.

"Also, I didn't think you'd agree to let us join you." While Milady addressed the entire group at once, the comment obviously was directed at Athos, who'd been glowering at the girls ever since they'd arrived.

"And for good reason," Athos said. "Ladies have no place on a journey such as this. It's far too dangerous, even with warriors like us along. Pursuing us on your own was pure foolishness. You're lucky to be alive."

Catherine bristled at this, though Milady simply shrugged off Athos's comment. "Oh, we can handle ourselves all right."

"You might have starved to death if you hadn't caught up to us, though," Athos said.

"It's not that hard to kill a rabbit if you have the time,"

Catherine said testily. "We simply didn't." To Greg, Catherine didn't look capable of killing a fly, but she spoke with such confidence that he wondered if he'd underestimated her.

"Still, you *did* put yourselves at risk," Aramis told the girls. "Why did you feel it was *so* necessary to join our mission?"

"Because I'm in charge of anything that has to do with Anne of Austria," Milady replied.

"Once she becomes the queen," Athos put in. "Until then, your allegiance is to France."

"I'm *here* because of my allegiance to France," Milady said curtly. "This wedding has been arranged to broker peace between France, Spain, and the Habsburgs. And now, less than two months before that is to take place, Spanish assassins make an assault on you just outside of Paris. I also understand that the messenger Dominic Richelieu sent me to meet was a Spanish emissary."

"That's correct," Aramis said.

"So if the Spanish are about to broker a peace, why are they infiltrating our country like this?" Milady asked.

"That's what the king sent *us* to find out," Athos said pointedly.

"Well, I'd like to know, too," Milady stated.

"Fine," Athos said. "Then go back to Paris and we'll tell you what's going on when we find out."

Milady fixed him with a hard stare. "We're not dead

weight, you know. We can contribute as much to this mission as you do."

"Two girls?" Athos snorted. "Not a chance."

"Do any of you speak Spanish?" Milady asked.

An uncomfortable silence fell over the Musketeers. "Do *you*?" Aramis asked.

"I wasn't given the job of handmaiden to the future queen simply for my charming personality," Milady said curtly. "Anne doesn't speak a word of French. *Pero hablo bien el español.*"

"What's that mean?" Athos asked.

"That I'm going to be able to get along much better in Spain by knowing the language than you are by wielding a sword," Milady replied. "What did you think you were going to do, barge around the country waving your weapons until everyone suddenly learned to speak French?"

Even Aramis reddened at the insult to their plan. "We felt we could get by," he explained. "I can speak Latin. Spanish derives from it, just as French does."

"Latin will serve you well if you find yourselves in ancient Rome," Milady said. "But you're going to *Spain*. Catherine and I can both speak the language. You need us."

The Musketeers all looked from one to the other. Aramis was practically beaming with joy now that Milady had made her case for joining their mission—and Porthos was never one to turn down female companionship. As for Greg, he was pleased to have the girls along as well, and not merely because he found Catherine attractive; having two more people along made him feel safer.

He glanced at Athos, who was frowning, the lone hold-out. Greg knew Athos didn't trust Milady. But even Athos seemed to recognize that Milady had made a solid argument for coming along—and that no one else would agree to send her home again. "Fine," he said grudgingly. "But be warned, this isn't going to be some fancy excursion."

"I'd already figured that out." Milady waved toward the roasted rabbits as evidence.

"Well, this is downright cushy compared to how things are going to be," Athos cautioned. "I suspect you know that René Valois is linked to those assassins who came after us the other day?"

Milady nodded, taking another bite of the rabbit.

"Well, Valois still has friends in Paris. If you could figure out where we've gone, Valois will figure it out, too. Which means we could have those assassins on our tail soon, if they aren't already."

"I'm aware of that," Milady said coolly.

"That's not all," Athos went on. "The closer we get to Spain, the more dangerous it becomes—whether you know the language or not. I can't afford to have anyone slowing us down. The purpose of this mission is to serve the king. Whoever jeopardizes it gets left behind."

Milady tossed a well-gnawed bone aside. "Whatever happened to 'All for one and one for all'?"

"That applies to the Musketeers, not hangers-on," Athos replied. "The members of our team have all proven themselves in battle."

Milady held his stare across the flames for a long moment. It was challenging, but Greg thought he might have noticed a glimmer of respect in it as well. "Fine," she said. "Understood."

Athos shifted his gaze to Catherine.

"Understood," she repeated.

Neither she nor Milady seemed fazed by the idea of danger, which surprised Greg. Athos's speech, which was meant to frighten the girls, had done the job on him instead. He still feared that *he* might turn out to be dead weight. What if he jeopardized the mission? Would the Musketeers actually leave him behind—or was that just a bluff?

The meal was done now, and Athos and Porthos set off into the woods to bury the rabbit bones so the smell wouldn't attract wolves to the campsite. Aramis went to check the supplies, leaving Greg with the girls.

It was his first chance to see Milady alone since she'd told him she needed to speak to him.

"Milady, I was wondering if we might speak privately." Greg looked at Catherine warily, and Milady nodded to dismiss her. Once she was out of earshot, Greg continued. "When I saw you in the throne room the other day, you said you had found something of Dominic's that you wanted to show me. . . ."

"Yes, I apologize for not finding you sooner. I do have something to show you . . . although there's something I wanted to talk to you about first. I'm very interested in your connection to Dominic Richelieu."

Greg felt a slight chill go through him. "What do you mean?"

Milady finally turned to face him, her eyes glowing in the firelight. "Do you think that, just because I'm a lady, I'm a fool?"

"No. Of course not."

"Then don't treat me like one. I have great loyalty to the king and future queen, and therefore I make it my business to stay abreast of anything suspicious that may be of danger to them. And you and your family are very suspicious. You arrived suddenly in the palace just over two months ago. To this day, no one knows how you got in. And then, at the very same time, Dominic began to act very differently."

"How do you mean?" Greg asked.

"For one thing, there were suddenly two of him," Milady said.

Greg let the statement hang there for a moment, unsure what his response ought to be. "That's his twin brother," he said finally.

"I never heard of Dominic having a twin before he suddenly showed up," Milady said.

"That doesn't mean it isn't possible," Greg said.

"No," Milady admitted. "But there's something strange about this twin, wouldn't you say?" She looked Greg directly in the eye, challenging him.

"Yes, there *is* something strange about Dominic's twin," Greg agreed. "But I don't know what it is."

"That's very disappointing," Milady said. She took a few steps toward Greg, keeping her eyes locked on his, until they were less than a foot apart. "I was hoping you'd be of more help. You're not the only one here charged with protecting the royal family, you know. But rest assured, I intend to find out what is going on with Dominic—and what your family's connection is to all of it."

Staring into Milady's eyes, Greg suddenly felt himself wanting to tell her everything. *Why was it so important to keep everything a secret?* he wondered. It'd feel good to get it all out in the open. And yet, he had this nagging feeling that, for some reason, he shouldn't trust her. . . .

"Am I interrupting something?"

Greg turned and found Aramis standing close by. He was staring at the two of them, trying to be casual about finding them so close together, but obviously quite jealous.

"No!" Greg scrambled to come up with a suitable lie. "We were just talking about, uh . . ."

"This." Milady produced a folded piece of parchment from her clothes. "I was about to call you over to discuss it as well." She lied with such ease that Greg almost believed her himself.

"What is it?" Aramis came and took the parchment.

"It belonged to Dominic, I believe," Milady replied.

Aramis and Greg examined the parchment in the firelight. It was a rough map of Paris: only the outline of the city wall was drawn on it, along with some wavy lines to represent the Seine and a small oval for the Île de la Cité. There were several strange marks on it, however. Three random points on the wall were indicated with arrows. And beneath the Île de la Cité was an odd collection of symbols:

Το στέμμα της Μινέρβας

"Where did you find this?" Aramis asked. "We searched Dominic's office and living quarters a dozen times over after he was imprisoned."

"Not well enough, apparently," Milady said. "Although I'm not the one who found it." She pointed across the campfire to Catherine, who had wandered close again. "*She* is."

Greg and Aramis shifted their gaze to Catherine, who shrank, as though uncomfortable being the center of attention. "A few days ago, I was told to clean out Dominic's office," she explained. "It's being given to someone else. And while I was cleaning, I noticed a loose stone in the wall. When I pressed on it, it slid aside, revealing a secret compartment. This was inside. I thought it might be important, so I took it to Milady."

"And that's when I contacted you, D'Artagnan," Milady said.

Aramis turned on Greg, suspicious. "You never said Milady had approached you."

"I didn't realize she wanted to talk to *all* of us," Greg explained. "The entire exchange lasted only a second."

Aramis frowned, as though he didn't necessarily believe that, then returned his attention to the map. "What is this?" he asked, pointing to the strange inscription beneath the Île de la Cité.

"I have no idea," Milady admitted. "I was hoping you'd know."

Aramis frowned at the marks and shook his head. "No. They merely look like mystic runes to me." He turned to Greg hopefully. "Any ideas?"

Greg shook his head sadly. "I've never seen anything like it. It looks a tiny bit like hieroglyphics. . . ."

"The language of the Egyptians?" Aramis asked, intrigued.

"Yes, but as far as I know, that's all actual symbols, like birds and eyeballs and things," Greg told the others. "I don't know what these are."

"Another code, perhaps," Aramis said with a sigh.

Another code? Greg thought, remembering how much the one in his great-grandfather's diary had stymied him. *Why can't anyone just write down what they actually mean and make life easy for once?*

"And what do you think *these* indicate?" Catherine asked. She pointed to one of the three small arrows marking spots on the city wall.

"They're secret passages into the city," Athos said.

Everyone jumped, startled. They wheeled around to find that Athos had come silently up behind them. Now he regarded the others coldly, as though annoyed they'd convened without alerting him.

"Secret passages?" Aramis was stunned. "I've never heard of any secret passages into the city."

"That's what makes them secret," Athos chided. "They're only known by certain members of the military."

"Why would anyone build secret passages into Paris?" Greg asked.

"In case the city was ever conquered," Athos explained. "If an enemy took Paris, they would only defend the gates. But if there's a way around the gates, a liberating force could sneak back inside and take the enemy by surprise."

"But *our* army only defends the gates," Aramis protested. "If an enemy knew about these entrances, *they* could sneak into the city as well."

"That's why they're supposed to be secret," Athos explained. "I only knew about the location of this one." He pointed to the arrow on the southern side of the city. "Dominic Richelieu obviously knows of two more."

"And now he's allying himself with Spain," Aramis said.

Silence descended as everyone grasped what this meant.

Finally, Milady voiced what they were all thinking. "He's going to help Spain invade Paris."

Greg felt as though he'd been punched in the stomach. "So what do we do now? Send a pigeon back with the news?"

"I think that'd be wise . . ." Aramis began.

"No, it'd be a waste of a valuable pigeon," Athos argued. "We're merely guessing that's what Dominic intends to do."

"It's a very educated guess," Aramis countered.

"But a guess nonetheless," Athos told him. "And even if we're right, we don't know how he plans to invade—or when. Or with what size force. Alerting the king before we know any of this serves no purpose."

"He could seal the tunnels," Aramis shot back.

"If we knew exactly where they were," Athos said hotly. "But we don't. We only know that *Richelieu* knows where they are."

"Perhaps the king knows of them," Aramis said. "Or one of his military advisors . . ."

"And what if we're wrong?" Athos demanded. "Then the entrances will be sealed and of no use should we ever truly need them."

"You'd rather have them be used against us?" Aramis asked accusingly.

"We are not sending a pigeon!" Athos roared, so loud that his voice echoed through the forest. "Not until we have found Dominic and Michel and determined once and for all, what they are truly up to! To do anything else would be rash and stupid!"

He spun on his heel and stormed off into the night, leaving everyone else stunned by his outburst.

Greg turned to Aramis. His fellow Musketeer was angrier than Greg had ever seen him, seething with rage over the way Athos had spoken to him. "Protecting the crown is not stupid," he spat, then stormed off as well.

Greg watched him disappear into the darkness, feeling like he was teetering on an abyss himself. If the Musketeers were going to have such a big argument over merely sending a pigeon to the king, what would happen when the stakes were life and death?

To his surprise, Catherine was suddenly beside him. "Do you think it's possible," she whispered, "that Dominic could really be planning an attack on Paris?"

"I think anything is possible," Greg replied sadly. It now seemed that Michel and Dominic were determined to alter the history of the world—and Greg feared that the Musketeers might not last as a team to stop it.

TEN

THREE DAYS LATER, THE MUSKETEERS ENCOUNTERED THE first hostile village.

It sat on the banks of the Saône River, a tributary that flowed to the Rhône and eventually to the south of France. At first, Greg was thrilled to see the town. After a week traveling in the forest, any sign of civilization was a sight for sore eyes. From a distance, it appeared picturesque as could be, straight out of a storybook.

As they grew closer, however, Greg found it far less attractive. The buildings were little more than hovels, with patchy roofs and collapsing walls. Unlike the cobblestone streets of Paris, the roads were rutted dirt tracks often reduced to mud.

The residents didn't look much better. Gaunt and pale, their faces were caked with dirt, their hair was stringy and matted, and their clothes were more holes than fabric. Worst of all, many had small, bloated pustules on their bodies.

Greg had expected that, in a remote town like this, people would have been thrilled to have visitors. Instead, everyone glowered at them with their sunken eyes.

"What's wrong with them?" Greg whispered to Aramis.

"You've never seen Black Death before?" Aramis responded.

The plague! Greg recoiled in his saddle, suddenly wanting to get as far from this town as possible. He knew from history class that the plague had wiped out millions of people in Europe in the 1300s, over half the population in some places. But he didn't know that it had still been around after that. He clapped his hand over his mouth, afraid to even breathe the air. "Is this common in the countryside?"

"I have no idea," Aramis admitted. "Luckily, Paris has been spared of late. We haven't had an outbreak for almost a decade."

Greg shuddered. Now, every prick at his skin made him quiver, fearful that it might be a plague-bearing flea. "Why do they seem so unhappy to see us?"

"Because they don't trust outsiders. Many people suspect the plague was brought to them by travelers."

Greg swallowed. For once, people of this time weren't wrong about something scientific. At some point, some infected traveler probably *had* brought the plague to this town. "But we couldn't possibly make them *more* sick," Greg protested. "If anything, we could get infected by *them*."

"They're not taking any chances," Aramis said. "No one knows what causes the plague, so people shun plenty of things: full moons, black cats, children born with strange birthmarks. You've remarked before that people of our time are overly superstitious? This is why. There is so much that is unknown, so much to fear in their lives."

The town wasn't large. It took only a few minutes to pass through the heart of it, although Greg, uneasy from the glares of the plague victims, felt like it took ten times as long. On the far side, a small, rickety dock with a few boats tied to it extended into the river—although only one boat actually appeared seaworthy. It was a small barge, wide and flat and completely open to the elements, but it was big enough for the entire party and it had a mast with a tattered sail.

Porthos pointed to it and addressed the entire town. "Who here owns that boat? We'd like to purchase it."

There was silence. Finally, a young man stepped forward. "We have no desire to do business with representatives of the king. The last ones who came through here robbed us blind."

Greg exchanged an intrigued look with the other Musketeers, all of them thinking the same thing at once. "Was this around two months ago?" Aramis asked. "Was one of the men very tall, with long black hair—and a missing hand?"

Many of the townsfolk reacted with surprise. "Yes," the man admitted. "But there were *two* men like that. Twins, one with a hand and one without."

"Those were not true representatives of the king," Athos told the crowd. "They are imposters and enemies of France. In fact, we have been dispatched by the king to find them and dispense justice. What did they do to you?"

There were some murmurs through the crowd. Finally, another man stepped forward. He was healthier-looking than most of the others, his arms thick with muscles from a lifetime of hard work. "They stole my boat," he said. "I'm a fisherman, and I had the finest craft in town. They asked me to sell it, but I refused. It was my livelihood. So they used black magic on me."

"Black magic?" Greg asked, incredulous. "What happened?"

"The one without the hand put me to sleep," the fisherman replied. "He got off his horse—I thought he was going to *talk* to me—but then he grabbed me and placed a magic cloth over my face. The next thing I knew, it was nighttime. I'd been asleep for hours and my boat was long gone." He shot an angry glance at the rest of the townsfolk.

"The men threatened to do the same to all of us if we stood against them," the young man explained defensively. "We didn't know he was asleep. We thought he'd been killed by mere touch."

"I *did* try to stop him," a man with a scraggy beard said. "But he threw fire at me and made a pigsty explode!"

The Musketeers and the girls reacted with alarm. Aramis looked to Greg for help. "The guards at the Bastille said something similar after Dinicoeur freed Richelieu. That he could put men to sleep by touching them and make walls explode with a simple gesture. What do you make of it?"

"Where is this pigsty?" Greg asked.

The bearded man pointed to a spot a few yards away. There was a small blast crater in the ground.

Greg dismounted his horse and went to inspect it. He could feel the eyes of the entire town on him. The people seemed to be unsure if he were brave or foolish for entering a place where magic had been used. Apparently, no one else had dared approach this spot since the explosion; the charred remains of the wooden sty were still scattered about.

Greg knelt by the crater. In the center of it was half of a metal casing, about the size of a baseball. It had apparently been blown in two. The other half was nowhere to be seen.

"He didn't throw fire," Greg told the Musketeers. "He threw a grenade."

"A grenade?" Aramis asked.

"A small explosive," Greg explained. "A metal casing filled with gunpowder. Dinicoeur just had to light it and throw it and it'd blow up whatever it hit. It's definitely not magic."

"How about the ability to put men to sleep?" Athos asked.

"Not magic either," Greg replied. The fisherman's mention of the "magic cloth" had helped him figure it out. "He used chloroform, a chemical that can be used to knock people unconscious." Greg strained to remember a class lecture on chemistry the year before. "Dinicoeur must know how to make it. If you put a little on a cloth, and press that to someone's face so that they're forced to inhale it, they'll fall asleep."

"Sure sounds like black magic to *me*," Porthos said.

Athos returned his attention to the townsfolk. "We are not like the others who passed through here before. We are honorable men who serve the crown. If you sell us your boat, we can find these traitors and avenge the terrible deeds they perpetrated here."

To his surprise, the fisherman laughed derisively. "Do you take us for fools? You'll never catch them. They have a two-month head start on you!"

"We have tracked them this far," Aramis said. "And we have a good idea where they are going. Now, we need that boat. The fate of our country hangs in the balance."

"The fate of *your* country, perhaps," said a diseased-looking woman. "Our town has had nothing but ill fortune since Louis took the throne."

"I assure you, your king is not responsible for any of your misfortune," Milady announced. "He has only your best interests at heart."

"Ha!" The woman spat on the ground. "He may be *your* king, but he's not mine."

The rest of the village responded in kind, with hoots and catcalls.

"If you do not respect the king, then perhaps you will respect a good deal," Porthos said. "We will trade our horses for that boat."

Silence fell over the crowd. The other Musketeers and the girls wheeled on Porthos, startled by his offer. "Are you insane?" Athos hissed angrily. "We'll need these horses to get to Spain!"

"And how do you propose to get them on that boat?" Porthos replied.

Athos looked back at the boat and frowned, realizing Porthos had a point.

The young man stepped forth again. "No matter what you offer, we have no interest in selling that boat to the likes of you."

The other villagers responded with hoots and catcalls again.

Except for one. A gnarled old man emerged from his home. "Speak for yourselves," he snapped at the crowd. "That's my boat, not yours." Cautiously, he approached the Musketeers and examined the horses, running his hands over their bodies, feeling the muscles underneath. He took Greg's horse by the reins, stared into its eyes and then checked its teeth. Finally he nodded with satisfaction. "These are good, healthy steeds, and I can always build another boat. I'll take you up on your offer."

"Excellent!" Porthos said. "Then six of them are yours." He pointed to the fisherman. "The others are for you, as restitution for the boat that was stolen."

The fisherman beamed. "Perhaps we have misjudged the crown," he said.

Although Aramis and Athos were annoyed with Porthos for offering the horses, now that the deal had been offered, there was no rescinding it—and they needed the boat. The trade was made, and Greg and the others loaded their gear onto the barge and set off down the river.

As the plagued village faded into the distance, Milady turned to Porthos and asked, "Once we reach the end of the river, exactly how do you plan to get to Spain without horses?"

Porthos shrugged. "We'll have to fall off that bridge when we come to it."

"Don't you mean 'cross that bridge'?" Milady asked.

"Whatever." Porthos propped his back on a sack of gear,

stuck his arms behind his head and sighed contentedly. "I say we just enjoy this while we can. Beats the daylights out of sitting in a saddle all day."

"You're a fool," Milady told him.

"Perhaps, but at least I'm a fool with a boat." Porthos laughed, tipped his hat over his eyes, and soon fell asleep.

ELEVEN

GREG SNAPPED AWAKE IN THE MIDDLE OF THE NIGHT, FEEL-ing as though he was freezing to death. His teeth were chattering and his fingers were numb. As he wrapped his arms around himself, he discovered that his clothes were soaking wet.

Greg's fear quickly gave way to annoyance. He looked down at where he'd been sleeping. Sure enough, water had oozed through the planks in the barge, pooling around him while he'd slept. Now the night winds blow-ing down the river had combined with his damp clothes to chill him to the bone.

He fumbled around the barge, looking for a dry blanket. In the inky darkness of the moonless sky, he could barely make out the forms of the other five passengers. Everyone else was asleep. Which was a problem, given that Porthos was supposed to be on watch.

Now Greg felt himself growing angry. It wasn't hard to pick Porthos out from the sleeping bodies; his snoring was as loud as a jet engine. Before Greg even realized he was doing it, he'd booted Porthos in the leg.

"Huh?" The portly Musketeer struggled to open his bleary eyes. "D'Artagnan? Is that you?"

"Yes," Greg hissed. "You're supposed to be on watch. Seeing as Valois and the assassins might be plotting to ambush us again."

"I am?" Porthos wasn't conscious enough to register concern. "Well, as long as you're awake, why don't you take over for me? I'm beat." He closed his eyes, and, to Greg's astonishment, was snoring again within seconds.

Another cold breeze made Greg shiver. He quickly peeled off his wet shirt and wrung it out. It seemed like half a gallon of water poured out of it. Greg realized he must have been pretty exhausted himself to sleep through a soaking that bad, but then, life on the river had been far more exhausting than anyone had expected.

They'd all expected it to be easy: The current and the wind would carry them downstream, and all they'd have to do was steer now and then. Unfortunately, the barge had been built for short trips and wasn't nearly as seaworthy as everyone had hoped, and it didn't steer well at all. In fact, it seemed to have a mind of its own, either heading for the most treacherous parts of the river, which could be terrifying, or the slowest. The Musketeers had spent two hours that day shoving the barge off a mud bank. Twice.

In addition, there was no shade on the barge. The days out on the open water, under the direct heat of the summer sun, were broiling and sapped everyone's energy. By nightfall, everyone was usually worn out and desperate for bed—only, getting a full night's sleep on the barge was virtually impossible. It pitched and yawed wildly, and as Greg had just learned for the umpteenth time, it also leaked.

Despite all this, however, the worst thing about traveling on the river was that it exacerbated everybody's conflicts.

When all six of the travelers had been on horseback, they'd been free to spread apart at times. But that was impossible on the barge. Instead, arguments tended to start over the smallest issues and flare up into major blowouts. After three days on the river, everyone was testy and peevish.

The only respite came when food ran low. Every afternoon, when the sun was at its worst out on the open water, they would dock the barge on the side of the river and search for provisions. At these times, Athos and Porthos would head off to hunt while everyone else combed the woods for edible plants. After an hour, they would all return with what they'd found. Greg always hoped that everyone's spirits would be refreshed after their time alone, but it was never long before an argument broke out again. And so everyone had begun to keep to themselves, carving out their own personal spaces on the barge as it drifted downstream.

Greg finally came across a blanket that was, by some miracle, mostly dry. He wrapped it around himself and finally stopped shivering. Then he plunked himself on the deck and looked out at the riverbank, casing it for assassins.

Not that he'd even be able to see them. The riverbank was pitch-black, and the assassins weren't going to be carrying torches. And yet everyone felt that they couldn't drop their guard completely. Someone had to stand watch every night.

Greg found Aramis's rucksack and dug around in it until he came across the map Milady had brought to them—Richelieu's map of Paris—and made yet another attempt to decipher the strange runes on it. He'd done this before. In fact, he'd done it every time he'd had the night watch, to no avail. He couldn't make any sense out of them. His first thought was that it had been a cryptogram, a simple code where one symbol stood for A, another stood for B, and so on, but two nights before, he'd tried every combination he could think of and nothing worked. So what did it mean? Why was it half letters and half weird symbols? To Greg's frustration, he had a nagging sense that he'd seen some of these symbols before, but he couldn't place where or when. If he could just remember that, it seemed, he could figure out what the inscription meant, but try as he might, he kept coming up blank.

The sound of a twig snapping echoed across the water.

Greg swiveled toward the riverbank, searching for whatever had made the sound, wondering if he should wake the others. To his surprise, day was beginning to break. Even though the sun was a good fifteen minutes from poking over the horizon, the sky to the east was lightening.

Greg couldn't see anything moving on the riverbank, but twigs didn't just snap, did they? Something must have been out there. He reached toward Athos, only to discover his fellow Musketeer already awake. His eyes were wide-open, riveted on the riverbank.

"Did you hear that?" Greg whispered to him.

Athos sat up and nodded. "Someone's watching us from shore."

"Do you think it's the assassins?"

"I'm guessing it's not."

"Why?"

"Because no one's tried to kill us yet." Athos stiffened suddenly. "What's that?"

It took a moment for Greg to see what Athos had. Up ahead, at a bend in the river, a large oak tree was marked with a bright slash of white.

Greg suddenly got the sense that someone else on the boat was awake. He spun toward the others. Everyone else was still out—although Greg felt that, just possibly, Milady had snapped her eyes shut just as he'd turned around. He was leaning toward her, trying to tell if she was merely pretending to sleep . . .

. . . when Athos sprang to his feet behind him, grabbed the rudder, and began to steer the barge toward the oak.

Greg turned toward him, forgetting all about Milady. "What are you doing? You think there's someone watching us, and you're heading *toward* them?"

"I'd rather confront my enemies than wait for them to attack," Athos replied.

"Okay, that's your choice. But there are other people on this boat who might not agree."

"This is for all of our benefit, D'Artagnan. Trust me."

Greg decided to wake the others to let them have a say but found they had all been roused by the conversation.

"What's going on?" Catherine asked, blinking in the dawn light. "Why are we so close to shore?"

Athos answered before Greg could. "Someone's keeping an eye on us, and I intend to find out who."

"What?" Porthos gasped. "Are you insane?"

A second later, the barge grounded in the shallows of the river, coming to a stop so quickly that everyone was thrown to the deck. Athos sprang into the thigh-deep water and raced to shore, despite everyone's shouts for him to stop.

Before Greg knew what he was doing, he'd grabbed his damp shirt and his sword and followed. The others were right on his heels.

Greg caught up to Athos at the shoreline. The swordsman was staring at the white mark on the oak tree. It was part of a larger artwork that had been carved deep into the trunk: a white rose. Someone had put a great deal of work into it, carefully etching the stem and leaves, then painting the petals white.

"What on earth is this?" Athos asked.

"Do you know *anything*?" Aramis snapped. "The white rose is the insignia of the Prince of Condé."

Catherine gasped in surprise. "What's it doing here?"

"Marking his territory," Aramis replied. "Apparently, it's been put here as a message to anyone heading down the river that these lands are loyal to him."

Greg felt himself fill with concern and noticed his fellow travelers reacting similarly—except Athos, who seemed offended by the mark of the rose. "Condé is not the ruler of this country," the swordsman growled. "The king is." Brandishing his weapon, he stormed into the woods.

The others had no choice but to go after him. Greg fell in beside Aramis as they moved through the forest. "How can these lands be loyal to someone who isn't the king?" he whispered.

"It's not unusual," Aramis confided. "France, just like any country in Europe, isn't a nation so much as a loosely allied patchwork of lands—and the people don't always agree on who should be king. Much of this country didn't support Louis's father, Henry, when he took the throne; thousands of his supporters were massacred in protest."

"By their fellow Frenchmen?" Greg asked, aghast.

"Yes," Aramis said, sounding ashamed. "And Louis probably has even less support than his father did, because he was only a child when he took the throne."

"So . . . all those people want Condé to be king?"

"Oh no. Not at all. Although, we've obviously entered an area that supports him. But other parts of the country support other men. Most people are far more beholden to their local royalty than to the king. They have never seen King Louis and probably never will. What he does in Paris ultimately has little effect on them."

"And yet there are many people willing to fight wars over who is king," Greg said.

"True," Aramis admitted sadly. "All too true."

They burst through a copse of trees and nearly stumbled over Athos. He was crouched on the ground, examining a set of footprints in the mud. "It was only three men," he announced, then turned and pointed to the river, which wasn't far through the trees. "They were watching us from here, but they turned and headed inland, rather than coming to face us."

"So, it wasn't the assassins?" Porthos asked hopefully.

"No," Athos replied. "These men were wearing different

shoes from the man D'Artagnan killed. I suspect we don't have anything to worry about from them. They were probably frightened off when they saw us." He proudly flourished his sword.

"Or perhaps they went off to get reinforcements," Aramis cautioned. "I'd suggest we get back on the boat. This area is obviously hostile to representatives of the king."

"I agree." Greg turned back to face the rest of the group and gasped. "Where's Milady?"

The others realized, with shock, that Milady was no longer with them.

"I thought she was right behind me," Catherine said worriedly. "She must have fallen behind while we were running through the woods."

"She can't be far," Aramis said. "Catherine and I will retrace our steps to the boat. Everyone else, fan out, in case she got lost." With that, he took Catherine's hand and plunged back into the woods the way they'd come.

"My eye, she's lost," Athos muttered under his breath, but he followed Aramis's instructions anyhow. Greg and Porthos did the same, spreading out into the forest and calling Milady's name.

Greg hadn't gone far before he began to question their decision. In his concern over Milady, Aramis seemed to have forgotten about the men who'd been spying on them. What if he'd been right and they'd gone to get backup? Even if they hadn't, the Musketeers were now split up;

Greg doubted he could handle himself against three men at once. What would happen if he ran into men loyal to Prince Condé . . . ?

There was a flash of gold in the woods ahead. It was far away, but Greg could have recognized the color of Milady's hair anywhere. Something was strange, though. Despite the fact that everyone was yelling her name, Milady was moving *away* from them all. Greg shouted to her as well, but she didn't even look back. Instead, she seemed to step up her pace and disappeared into the trees.

Greg raced after her in the direction he thought she'd gone, but after a few minutes he stopped, fearing he'd made a mistake. He was getting too deep into the forest. Milady must have turned back, and he'd missed her somehow. . . .

Then he saw her.

Beyond a stand of trees, a small waterfall spilled into a crystal pool. Milady stood beside it.

Greg started to call out her name again but caught himself. There was something strange about Milady's behavior. She was looking about furtively, as if trying to determine if anyone had followed her. Reflexively, Greg crouched behind a bush and watched.

Had Athos been right to be suspicious about her? He thought back to the boat, just before Athos had steered for shore. Maybe she *had* in fact been awake, listening to them.

By the pool, Milady seemed convinced she was alone. She approached the waterfall and touched a rock beside it.

Greg couldn't see what she was doing with it, however, as his view was blocked by a tree. He quickly slunk closer.

Milady bent down and hitched up her dress to her calf, as though removing something she'd tucked inside her boot.

Greg, focused on the girl, stumbled over a stone. He caught himself quickly, barely making a rustle, but it was enough to alert Milady.

She spun around and screamed at the top of her lungs. "Help!" she cried. "Help me!" She sounded so convincing, Greg almost believed she *was* in trouble.

There was no point in trying to hide anymore. He emerged from the trees. "What were you just doing?" he demanded.

Milady actually seemed relieved to see him. "Oh, thank goodness it's you. I thought it was one of the assassins."

Greg looked at her, confused. "No, you didn't. I was watching you. . . ."

Milady gasped, offended. "You were spying on me?"

Before he could question this, Aramis came crashing through the woods with Catherine in tow. "Are you all right?" Aramis asked.

"No," Milady replied. "I caught D'Artagnan spying on me."

To Greg's surprise, Aramis and Catherine both wheeled on him accusingly. "That's not true!" he said.

"It certainly is," Milady snapped. "I was just about to bathe in this pool when I saw him—"

Porthos and Athos burst onto the scene from opposite directions. "What's going on here?" Athos demanded.

"D'Artagnan was watching Milady bathe," Aramis said coldly.

Porthos and Athos turned on Greg as well.

"I wasn't," Greg protested. "I stumbled upon her here. She was up to something." He turned on Milady. "Why would you be bathing in the middle of hostile territory?"

"Because I fell in the mud." Milady pulled up her dress again, revealing that her leg was caked with it. "I slipped while I was following everyone through the woods, and when I got back up again, you all had gotten ahead of me. I tried to find you, but I must have got turned around."

"You didn't hear us all yelling for you?" Greg asked.

"No. I suppose the waterfall was too loud." Milady waved at the pool of water. "Anyhow, when I came across this, I figured I could at least clean myself off quickly. I *thought* I was alone." She glared at Greg reproachfully.

Everyone else did the same.

Greg couldn't believe how quickly the tables had turned on him. He shook his head. "No, none of this is true. I think she was leaving a message for someone over here." He ran to the rocky face near the waterfall and ran his hands over the stones. One shifted under his touch. "Here it is!" He slid the stone aside, revealing a small space the size of a mailbox.

It was empty. There was no message hidden inside.

Greg's heart sank. He spun around to find everyone else glaring at him.

"That's enough of this foolishness," Aramis said disdainfully. "Let's allow Milady to wash the mud off herself and continue on our way. We are wasting time arguing."

"Thank you, Aramis," Milady said. "Your thoughtfulness is greatly appreciated."

Everyone else started into the woods to give Milady privacy. Greg glanced back at her, expecting that she might flash him a knowing smile, or some other indication that she'd one-upped him, but only got a cold stare in return. Doubt crept into his mind. Had he really misjudged her so badly?

Greg sighed. Even if Milady *had* been up to something, there'd be no convincing anyone else of it. She'd turned them all against him. They all seemed disgusted by his behavior. In addition to heading into hostile territory to confront a madman with assassins on his tail, Greg had now found a way to make things even worse.

He'd put his friendships in jeopardy.

TWELVE

GREG HOPED THAT THINGS MIGHT RETURN TO NORMAL
after the bathing incident, but they didn't.

Porthos had *tried* to act like nothing had happened, jok-
ing around as usual, but there was an awkwardness to it,
as though he didn't quite feel comfortable around Greg.
Still, that was better treatment than Aramis and Athos
gave him. For the first day afterward, both of them were
cold and removed around Greg, obviously upset at what
they believed he'd done. But after that at least the Musketeers talked to him again. The girls didn't. It wasn't

easy to avoid somebody on a small boat, but the girls did their best. Milady regarded him coldly and only spoke to him when she had to. Catherine barely acknowledged his presence.

So now the trip wasn't merely dangerous, it was also uncomfortable. Greg began to volunteer for the night shifts, limiting his time awake with everyone else to a minimum. The rest of the time he kept to himself, sitting on the edge of the boat, dangling his feet in the water, wishing he'd never followed Michel Dinicoeur back to 1615. He dreamed about finding the Devil's Stone and returning to his own time again.

And he kept an eye on Milady.

He still wasn't sure he hadn't truly stumbled upon her bathing, but he figured the best way to exonerate himself was to catch her doing something else. And yet she remained stubbornly well behaved. Over the next few days on the river, she did nothing suspicious in the slightest. Greg began to feel as though he must have made a mistake and misjudged her.

It was five days after the bathing incident before he finally had a normal conversation with someone.

It was late afternoon, and they had gone ashore. Athos and Porthos were hunting while the others foraged. Greg was busily picking blackberries when he rounded a patch of brambles and almost stumbled into Catherine.

The girl immediately flushed red in embarrassment.

"Oh! Sorry to bother you!" she said, and backed away, ready to leave.

"Wait! Please don't go." Greg said it so quickly he surprised himself.

It seemed to catch Catherine off guard as well. She hesitated a moment. "I really ought to—"

"I'm not as bad as you think I am," Greg said, a pleading tone in his voice. "That whole thing with Milady was just a misunderstanding."

Catherine wavered, then lowered her eyes. "I don't think you're bad at all," she said quietly.

"Really?" Greg asked.

"Really." Catherine kept her eyes rooted to the ground. "I just think you made a mistake. But I understand why, too. This trip . . . Heading into dangerous territory, worried assassins might attack . . . It makes sense to be on one's guard." She took a step back, as though she might leave, but then turned to the closest bush and began picking berries.

Greg returned to work himself, pleased that Catherine was even willing to be in his presence. But after a minute of this, he couldn't hold his silence any longer. "How are *you* doing?" he asked.

Catherine looked to him, curious. "What do you mean?"

"On the trip," Greg said. "Given the assassins and the danger and all. How are you doing with it?"

"Oh. Well . . ." Catherine hesitated before answering.

"Not that well, I suppose. It's quite stressful. I've never done anything like this. After all, I've only trained to be a handmaiden, not a Musketeer."

"It's not as though we've really trained for this either," Greg admitted.

"Well, it seems you've certainly trained for everything else," Catherine told him. "I've seen you practicing."

"You have?" Greg's heart sped up at this, which completely surprised him.

"Of course," Catherine said. "You're hard to miss, given that you spend several hours a day in the palace courtyard poking at things with your sword."

"Oh. Right. That makes sense." Greg racked his brain for something else to ask Catherine. "How long have you been working at the palace?"

"For as long as I can remember. My parents are both servants there."

"And so you had to become one?"

Catherine looked at Greg curiously. "Of course. How does it work in Artagnan with your servants?"

Greg almost said "What servants?" before he caught himself. He realized what Catherine's line of thought must be: Only someone wealthy could afford to travel to Paris. Thus, Greg must have money—and servants. "We, uh . . . we give them a choice as to whether to work for us or not," he said.

"A choice?" Catherine seemed confused by the very

concept. "But what else would they do?"

"Er . . . whatever they want," Greg said. "It's something new we're working on in Artagnan. We call it 'free will.'"

"Sounds dangerous," Catherine said.

Greg popped a few of the berries he'd collected into his mouth. "Haven't you ever thought about being something besides a servant?" he asked.

Catherine studied him cautiously before answering, as though this might be a trap. "I suppose, from time to time, I might have."

"And what might that be?"

"Well, being the queen doesn't seem too bad."

"Of course not. But, aside from royalty . . ."

"A soldier, I suppose."

Greg coughed on a berry. "A soldier? Really?"

Catherine's stare hardened. "You don't think a woman could be a soldier?"

"No! I mean yes," Greg stammered. "I mean, she could. It just seems, well . . . dangerous for a woman."

"So when you say your female servants can exercise free will, you mean only as long as they choose something safe, like being milkmaids?"

"No! I was just caught by surprise. That a girl as beautiful as you would want to be a soldier." Greg bit his lip, but it was too late. The word "beautiful" had slipped out . . . and Catherine had heard it.

She seemed taken aback, unsure how to respond. Her

cheeks flushed pink. But to Greg's relief, she pretended as though the word had never been spoken. "Why not?" she asked.

"Because it never seemed like much fun to me. Spending most of your time training—or on watch. The only time it's really exciting is when somebody tries to kill you."

"Maybe so. But then, as a member of the upper class, you're probably used to finding excitement other ways. For the rest of us, there's not much."

"Is that why you came on this journey?" Greg asked.

"I came because Milady requested that I accompany her," Catherine replied. "But should we encounter some excitement along the way, I suppose that would be all right."

"Why did Milady request *you*?" Greg was surprised how accusatory the question came out—but it had been on his mind ever since he'd first laid eyes on Catherine.

"I have no idea," Catherine said. "I suppose she heard I was a good and loyal servant."

For the first time in the entire conversation, Greg got the feeling Catherine was lying to him. "She didn't know you? I thought she was in charge of your training."

"No. The headmistress, who used to be chief hand-maiden to Louis's mother, oversees my training, although Milady *will* be my superior once Queen Anne arrives—or *if* she arrives, I suppose. In truth, I have only recently been selected to be a handmaiden. Before this, I was merely a cleaning girl in the quarters for the King's Guard."

"Hold on," Greg said. "You worked for Dominic Richelieu?"

"I work for the crown," Catherine replied. "Although I did clean Monsieur Richelieu's quarters. At least, I did until you ran him off."

Greg stared at Catherine for a while, trying to process this information. It couldn't have been a coincidence that, out of all the people Milady could have chosen to accompany her on this mission, she'd picked the very girl who'd worked for Richelieu. "Why didn't you ever mention this?" he asked.

"I thought Milady had already told you," Catherine said. "I did say that I had been asked to clean out his offices. . . ."

"But I never knew you worked so close to him. Did you ever encounter Michel Dinicoeur there?"

Catherine nodded. "Twice. He visited only when he thought Richelieu was alone, but people tend to overlook the servants sometimes."

"Are you the one who told Milady about him?"

Catherine considered that carefully. "Perhaps. I'm not sure. Why?"

Greg didn't answer right away. He wasn't even sure why he thought it was important, but somehow it seemed that it was. Instead, he asked the question that was burning inside him. "Did you, by any chance, ever hear Michel mention something called the Devil's Stone?"

Catherine's eyes widened in surprise, then narrowed in

suspicion. "How did you know about that?"

Greg's heart leaped with excitement. "What did you hear?"

Catherine responded by putting a finger to her lips and hushing him.

Something rustled in the bushes.

"It's probably just a squirrel," Greg whispered.

And then the thieves attacked.

THIRTEEN

THERE WERE THREE OF THEM, THEY WERE ALL VERY BIG, AND they moved with surprising speed. Within seconds, they had overwhelmed Greg, knocking him to the ground and wrenching his hands behind his back. The moment he tried to call for help, one crammed a rag in his mouth. Greg felt the cool steel of a knife blade pressed against his neck. "You'll stay still if you know what's good for you," his attacker hissed.

Greg obediently stopped struggling. He doubted he could have done anything anyhow. He'd foolishly left his sword on the barge.

The knife blade stayed against his flesh. "That's right," the man said. "And don't try calling to your friends, either. This is Prince Condé's territory. We don't take kindly to representatives of the king."

Greg wondered if these men were the ones who'd been watching the boat the other night. They appeared to be brothers; all had the same cruel look. The oldest, apparently the leader, had a scar angling across his nose from his left eye to the right side of his mouth. The next in line was the biggest, with broad shoulders and bulging muscles. The youngest was also the dimmest; he was slightly cross-eyed and the mere act of thinking seemed to cause him distress. Their clothing was poorly made and haphazardly stitched together. And they reeked as though they'd never bathed in their lives; Greg was surprised he hadn't been able to smell them from a mile away.

The thieves had little interest in Greg other than what valuables he might be carrying. However, they regarded Catherine as though she was a prize herself. While the middle one pinned her against a tree, the one with the scar stepped back to admire her.

"Look at her!" he crowed. "I've never seen clothes like these. What are you, darling, a princess?"

Catherine didn't respond. She just glared at the thieves, who weren't fazed a bit. "Hoo-hoo!" the scarred one laughed. "If you want to give us the silent treatment, that's fine by us."

Greg seethed with rage—although he was angrier with himself than the thieves. He'd made a terrible mistake by letting his guard down, and now Catherine was paying the price. He felt frightened and useless, unable to do anything but hope his friends came to their rescue.

His face was pressed into the ground, so he could barely see anything. He felt the muscular middle brother slice through his belt, then slide it off his body and remove the small pouch that held all his belongings.

"What's he got in there?" the scarred one demanded.

"Not much," his brother replied. "Just a few coins." He suddenly grew intrigued. "And *this* . . ."

"What on earth is that?" Greg heard the scarred one ask.

"I've never seen anything like it," the middle brother said. He jabbed Greg in the ribs with his boot. "Hey there," he demanded. "What is this thing?"

Greg lifted his head from the dirt and saw what the thief held in his grubby hands: Greg's cell phone.

Greg's heart skipped a beat. He couldn't lose his phone! He'd never get back to the future. But before panic could set in, he realized the phone might be able to get him out of this predicament.

"It's magic," he said.

The brothers—and Catherine—squinted at him skeptically, then at the phone. Greg knew it looked like nothing they'd ever seen before.

"What's it do?" the scarred one demanded.

"I have to show you," Greg said.

"Do I look like an idiot to you?" the scarred one snapped. "No way. Tell me how it works."

"I can't," Greg said. "It only works for me."

The thieves stepped back and conferred for a moment. Greg could hear snippets of their conversation: "It couldn't be magic. It's so small." "It *might*. It's very shiny." "What's it made of, silver?" In the end, curiosity won out, and he was released.

The middle brother jabbed the tip of his knife into Catherine's side, making her squeal. "Try anything funny and the princess here gets hurt," he warned.

Greg stood, brushed the dirt from his face, and reached for the phone.

The younger brother was suddenly behind him, wrapping a thick arm around his neck.

"Further incentive for you to not try anything funny," the scarred one warned. "My brother there can snap your neck in an instant, if I say so."

"Understood," Greg gasped. He could barely breathe with the arm pressed against his throat. His hands were trembling. He knew there was a decent chance that, if all didn't go the way he'd hoped right now, he'd end up dead. But then, if he did nothing, the thieves would probably kill him anyhow.

The scarred brother cautiously handed him the phone as the younger brother tightened his arm around Greg's neck.

Greg pressed the switch to turn the phone on. Even the background warm-up photo was enough to make the thieves gasp. It was just a picture Greg had snapped of a park in Queens near his apartment. But then, neither the thieves—nor Catherine—had ever seen a photograph before.

"Think that's impressive?" Greg asked. "You haven't seen *anything* yet." He flipped on the camera and aimed the phone at the scarred one. "Say cheese."

"Why?" the thief asked.

Greg snapped the picture, then brought it up on the screen and turned it to face the others.

The thieves recoiled in shock. Even Catherine went wide eyed.

"Is that *me*?" the scarred one demanded.

"Yes," Greg said.

"How did you get in that little box?" the middle brother asked, a bit frightened.

"It's only an image of him. Like a painting," Greg explained.

"Painted in a mere instant?" the scarred thief asked. "That's not possible."

"I told you," Greg said. "It's magic."

"I don't like it," the middle one said. "I hear sorcerers can do things like that. Steal men's souls."

While they were still in awe, Greg flipped to the music function and hit play, cranking the volume as high as it would go.

The phone picked a song at random and blasted it. It happened to be a noisy thrash metal song, and the sudden blare of electric guitars caught the thieves by surprise. As Greg had hoped, the cacophony of modern sounds was disorienting to them. Even better, none of the thieves could comprehend that the music was actually coming from the phone. Instead, they spun about, frightened, desperately looking for the musicians. The youngest one dropped his guard, relaxing his hold on Greg's neck.

Greg knew he wasn't going to get another chance. He grabbed the thief's fingers and yanked them back while simultaneously twisting free of his grip. While the younger thief howled in pain, Greg spun around and drove his knee into the thief's crotch, doubling him over. Then Greg snatched the thief's sword from his belt.

Catherine also snapped to action. Even though she was just as stunned by the music as the thieves, her survival instincts kicked in quickly. She pulled away from the middle brother and fled into the bushes.

Greg spun toward the middle thief, but the scarred one blocked Greg's sword with his own. "Go get her!" he ordered. "I can handle this one!"

The middle one did as he was told, plunging into the woods, as the scarred thief charged at Greg with his sword. The youngest thief staggered back to his feet, a knife in his hand. He was now moving gingerly, but he was still dangerous.

Greg parried their attacks, putting everything Athos had taught him to use. He was frightened, but he forced himself to calm down and remember Athos's instructions: *Stay in the moment. Focus. No matter how hard he tries not to, your attacker will always signal what he's going to do next. Predict, prepare—and counter.*

As their blades clanged against one another, Greg discovered something: He'd become quite good at sword fighting over the last two months. He hadn't realized it, because he'd been fighting Athos, who was as good as they came. But compared to the thieves, he was a pro. He saw their moves coming far in advance. Thus he deftly sidestepped each attack and kept them at bay.

He soon spotted an opening with the youngest thief, who was far less experienced than his brother. Greg brought the sword down across his arm, cutting a deep gash. The thief yelped in pain, dropped his knife, and abandoned the battle to stanch the bleeding.

Greg snatched the knife before the scarred one could, then took him on with both blades. Now that it was only man to man, he quickly overwhelmed the thief. He spun quickly, caught the blade of the other man's sword with his own, and sent it flying from his hand. As the scarred one gasped in surprise, Greg whacked him on the head with both hilts at once. The thief collapsed to the ground, unconscious.

Greg glanced at his phone. There was barely any battery

left. He quickly flicked it off to save what little power remained.

The song on the phone ended abruptly, and the woods went silent again, allowing Greg to hear Catherine's screams for help in the woods. He went after her.

She hadn't made it far. The middle thief had caught up to her in a clearing and tackled her in the grass. She was doing her best to fend him off, but he was overwhelming her with his sheer bulk. He stopped immediately, however, when Greg placed the blade of the sword against his neck.

"Get up," Greg ordered.

The thief spun around, surprised to see Greg there and not the others. "What did you do to my brothers?" he asked.

"I let them live," Greg said. "Though I might not be so understanding with you. Get away from the girl."

The thief stood quickly, his hands raised in surrender. Even though he was twice Greg's size, he now looked upon Greg with fear and respect. "We didn't mean nothing," he whined. "Please don't kill me."

"I'll think about it." Greg kept the sword against the thief's neck.

Catherine stood. Greg turned to her, expecting that she might throw herself into his arms, thankful for his valiant rescue.

But instead she looked even more afraid of him than the thief did. She glanced warily at the phone in Greg's hand, then fled—as though *he* was the dangerous one.

"Catherine!" Greg called. "Wait! I can explain!"

"Stay away from me, sorcerer!" she yelled as she disappeared into the woods.

The thief took advantage of the distraction to flee himself, running in the opposite direction. Greg didn't have the heart to chase him. Instead he stared after Catherine, realizing that he couldn't explain this at all. Anything he said would probably only frighten her even more.

There was a rustle from the bushes nearby. Greg spun around, sword raised, expecting another attack. Instead, he saw a glimpse of golden hair—Milady de Winter.

She vanished into the woods, leaving Greg to wonder why she was there, how much she'd seen—and what she was going to do about it.

FOURTEEN

AFTER THE ENCOUNTER WITH THE THIEVES, GREG couldn't get Catherine to talk to him again. He could barely get her to *look* at him—and when she did, he saw fear in her eyes. When the six travelers sat down to meals, she always made sure she was seated farthest away from Greg.

On the other hand, Milady now seemed to be keeping an eye on him. She was subtle about it, though. Greg would suddenly have the sense that she was watching him, although when he spun around, she was always looking somewhere else, albeit with a slight, knowing smile on her lips. Greg was tempted to just march up to her and demand to know what she'd seen, but he figured she'd somehow manage to turn that around and embarrass him in front of the other Musketeers again.

As for the Musketeers themselves, relations between them grew more and more strained as their travels continued.

Thus, Greg could barely contain his relief when, twelve agonizing days after first setting out on the river, the forest suddenly fell away from the riverbank, revealing a city in the distance.

"Arles," Aramis said. He—and everyone else—seemed to be thrilled that their time on the boat was finally at an end.

As they drifted toward the city, however, Greg's relief turned into astonishment. For a moment, he wondered if they'd somehow ended up in Italy. Arles looked nothing like Paris—or any of the small villages they had passed on their journey. Instead, it looked like a smaller version of Rome.

It was far larger than any other city they had encountered, more than twice the size of Paris itself. Many buildings were constructed in Roman style, featuring thick columns and intricate bas reliefs. The riverbanks were buttressed with stone and the roads were paved. An elaborate bridge crossed the Rhône, far more impressive than even the Pont Neuf in Paris, built upon pontoon boats so that it actually floated on the water, with towers and drawbridges at both ends. But most startling of all was the Arena. Perched on a hill above the river, it looked like a slightly smaller version of the Colosseum in Rome. Five stories tall and several blocks wide, it loomed above every other building in the city.

"This doesn't look like France," Greg said.

"Until recently, it *wasn't* France," Aramis explained. "It was founded by the Greeks over two thousand years ago. Then the Romans took it over and built it into what you see today. After that, it became the capital of its own country, the Kingdom of Arles, for a few hundred years. The area was only ceded to King Charles of France about a hundred fifty years ago."

Greg shook his head in amazement. He'd never had any idea that there were Roman cities in France. But then, Athos, Porthos, and the girls seemed surprised as well— and they *lived* in France. If anything, they were *more* astonished by the city.

"I'd always thought Paris must be the most beautiful city in the world," Milady said as they tied up the boat. "But now, compared to this place . . ."

"It looks like a cesspit," Porthos finished.

"That's not what I was going to say," Milady chided.

"Well, Paris certainly *smells* like a cesspit," Porthos taunted. "Whereas this town smells incredible." He inhaled deeply, relishing the smell—or lack of it—in the air. "There's no latrines in the streets! Where on earth do they put all their waste?"

"Underground," Aramis replied. "The Romans built a series of underground pipes, known as sewers, which use water to convey all human waste to the outskirts of the city. From what I understand, they also have an intricate system of pumps and aqueducts to bring fresh water to all the towns in this region." He pointed to a marble fountain that sat at the end of the pier. Fresh, clean water spurted from the mouths of carved fish and cherubs into a wide basin, where residents filled buckets for their daily use. It was a beautiful structure—and Greg couldn't help noticing that the residents of Arles looked considerably cleaner and healthier than those of Paris.

"It's a shame we won't be able to stay here long," Catherine said sadly.

"Well, we might be here at least a day or two," Porthos said. "We have to acquire horses and provisions—and it might be wise to seek some information while we're here as well. If this is the jumping-off point for Spain, then it's likely that this is where Dominic jumped off."

"I agree with Porthos," Aramis said.

"Then you're both fools," Athos snapped. "We can't afford to squander a day or two in our pursuit. . . ."

"Seeking the correct information isn't wasteful," Aramis shot back. "We have no idea which route they took from here. Starting our pursuit quickly means nothing if we head in the wrong direction."

"We know the right direction," Athos snarled. "Toward Spain. We don't need to waste precious time figuring that out."

"There are other things we ought to learn besides the mere direction they went," Aramis said. "Anyone with half a brain should know that."

Athos began to argue, but Milady stepped between the boys before he could. "You know what's *really* wasting our time? Your bickering. So Aramis and I are going to go find out if anyone has seen Dominic. . . ."

"Why the two of you?" Athos asked, failing to hide his jealousy.

"Because he speaks the most languages and I'm the most persuasive. The rest of you, find horses and supplies." Milady wheeled around and stormed down the pier.

Aramis shot Athos a gloating grin, then scurried after her.

"I wasn't saying that asking for information was a bad idea," Athos muttered. "Only that we shouldn't waste too much time doing it."

Porthos put a friendly arm around Athos's shoulders. "What say you and I take care of the horses? Greg and Catherine can handle the supplies." With that, he gave Greg a sly wink.

Greg could feel himself turning red in embarrassment. At the same time, Catherine went white. "Oh," she said. "I don't think that's such a good idea."

"Of course it is!" Porthos told her. "Athos and I are best suited to acquire horses. Athos knows the most about horses—and I know how to get the best bargain."

"You?" Catherine asked. "You traded our horses for a boat!"

"And now, I can probably trade that boat for some horses." Porthos leaned in to Greg and whispered, "Figured I'd give you both a little alone time to work out whatever's gone sour between you two. You can thank me later." Then he dragged Athos down the pier before anyone else could protest.

Catherine studied Greg for a moment, then bolted up the pier herself, as though afraid to be left alone with him.

"Catherine, wait!" Greg raced after her and caught her arm. "I can explain everything."

"I *understand* everything." Catherine struggled to pull away from him. "You can do magic, which is a dark art. . . ."

"It wasn't magic! Where I'm from, everyone can do what I did."

"Then Artagnan must be a terrible place. Now let me go or I'll scream."

"I'm not from Artagnan. I'm from the future!" Greg blurted out.

Catherine stopped struggling and simply stared at Greg in shock.

"That's not possible," she said, shaking her head.

"Trust me, it is," Greg told her. And before she could

protest, he told her everything: about the Devil's Stone, and how Dominic and Michel were really the same man, and how he and his parents had been sucked back through time. Once he started talking, he couldn't stop himself, and to be honest, he didn't want to stop. It was a relief to finally tell someone besides Aramis.

Catherine didn't say a word the whole time. She just stared at him, eyes wide with a mixture of fear and concern. When he finished, she sat at the edge of the fountain and shook her head.

"Do you believe me?" Greg asked.

"I don't know," Catherine admitted. "It all seems so bizarre . . . and yet, it also explains so much. About you—and Dinicoeur and Richelieu in particular. Certain things they said now make sense."

"What do you mean?"

"Well, Dinicoeur said that all his plans weren't for him, but for Richelieu—and that Richelieu had better take good care of himself, as his body really belonged to both of them." Catherine's eyes were alive now. Greg could sense that her mind was racing. "It's as though I've spent the last few months looking at a painting that's blurry and now it's suddenly becoming clear. It must be even more strange for you, yes?"

"'Strange' doesn't even begin to describe it," Greg said.

"How did the Musketeers react when you told them you were from the future?"

"Actually, only Aramis knows," Greg replied sheepishly. "I didn't think the others would believe it. Or that, if they *did* believe it, they'd still treat me the same way."

"Then why did you tell *me*?" Catherine asked.

"I guess I wanted you to know the truth about me," Greg admitted.

Catherine smiled, as though flattered. Her astonishment seemed to have subsided and was now replaced by curiosity. "So, that tiny box you had . . . Everybody in the future has one?"

"Almost everyone," Greg told her.

"And the horrible noise that came out of it. That's what music sounds like in the future?"

Greg laughed. "Not all of it. I think there's some you'd actually like."

"Really? Could you play me some?"

"I'd love to," Greg said. "But I can't. The battery is almost drained as it is."

"What's a battery?" Catherine asked.

"It's uh . . . this little metal thing that gives the box all its power. In the future it's easy to recharge, but there's no way to do it here. Once it's drained, the box won't work anymore. . . ."

"And then you won't be able to get home again," Catherine concluded.

"Yes."

"So . . . when you turned it on before, to frighten those

men in the woods, you were risking your future to protect me?"

"Uh, well . . . I guess," Greg said. "Although I have to admit, I was also trying to protect *myself*."

"Oh, I suspect that if I hadn't been held at knifepoint, you could have handled those men some other way." Catherine looked down at her feet. "I'm sorry I misjudged you."

Greg was still a bit surprised that being from the future made him less frightening to Catherine than someone who could work magic, but he guessed that, in a world ruled by superstition, someone who controlled the dark arts would be far more frightening than someone who had been a victim of them. "That's all right," he said. "I understand why you reacted the way you did."

Catherine smiled again. "I think you and I are supposed to be acquiring supplies," she said. And then, to Greg's surprise, she extended the crook of her arm to him.

Greg slipped his hand into it and the two of them set off into town.

Now that he'd told the truth about himself, Catherine quickly warmed to him, as if sharing his secret had bonded them closer. The tension that had been between them on the boat was gone. Instead, Catherine peppered him with questions about life in the future. She was fascinated by his tales of airplanes and televisions and video games. She was also thrilled to be in Arles, gasping with wonder at everything they passed: the intricate drawbridges over the river, a gorgeous bathhouse, a large outdoor amphitheater. Even the smallest architectural details elicited oohs and aahs from her.

They soon found the town's open-air market. It was in a wide plaza—far larger than the market square in Paris—with a soaring obelisk in the center. Now that it was the middle of summer, the stalls were spilling over with fresh produce. Greg and Catherine quickly set about purchasing some. For the first time in days, Greg found himself having fun, as though they were on vacation, rather than hunting down a madman. He almost hated to have to steer their conversation back to Dinicoeur.

"You asked before how I'd heard of the Devil's Stone," he told Catherine. "Well, now you know: It's what brought me here. And I need to find it again if I'm ever going to return home. So I have to know: What did you hear Michel Dinicoeur say about it?"

"It wasn't much, I'm afraid," Catherine replied. "It was the second time I heard him speak to Dominic. It didn't make sense to me at the time, but I realize now that they were discussing how Michel intended to make Dominic immortal. Michel said he needed to find the Devil's Stone, but it wouldn't be much trouble, because he'd done it once before and knew where both pieces of it were."

Greg's heart sank. "Wait. It's in two pieces now?"

"You didn't know? You said you had to put both pieces together to travel through time."

"Yes, but that was in the future. I thought that, maybe, it had been broken in two *after* Dominic had found it. Or at least, I was hoping that was the case. Did he say where the two pieces were?"

"He said the first was in Madrid . . . But as for the second, all he said was, it was right under the king's nose."

"You mean, the second half of the Devil's Stone is back in Paris?!" Greg shook his head. "This doesn't make sense. If half the stone is in Paris, why would Michel go all the way to Spain to get the other half first?"

"I don't know." Catherine lowered her eyes, as though ashamed. "I didn't hear the rest of the conversation. I was worried I'd be spotted, so I returned to my room. I'm sorry."

"There is nothing to apologize for," Greg said. "Did you ever tell Milady about this?"

Catherine gave him a sideways look. "What is it that you have against Milady?"

"I'm just not sure that I trust her," Greg admitted. "Do you?"

Catherine hesitated a second too long before answering. "She has never done anything I considered suspicious."

"She invited you to come on this journey, even though you barely knew her. Why?"

"She said she would require some assistance."

"Yes, but . . ." Greg tried to choose his words carefully. "She knew you were heading into hostile territory. In theory, it would have made sense to invite some soldiers along for protection. . . ."

"Rather than a mere handmaiden?" Catherine flushed, offended.

"But you're *not* a mere handmaiden," Greg said quickly. "You worked close to Dominic Richelieu. You *knew* things others didn't. I'm not saying it was a mistake to bring you. I just think it's odd that Milady brought *only* you . . . unless she wanted some time with you alone to try to find out what you knew."

Catherine's hard stare softened. She shook her head, as though upset with herself. "I have to admit, I asked myself some of the same questions. I even asked *her* if we should bring anyone along for protection, but she said our mission was a secret one and that we'd have your protection soon enough."

"Did she ask you about Richelieu and Dinicoeur?"

"Yes. But she always made it sound like small talk, not like she was prying for information."

"And did you ever tell her about the Devil's Stone?"

Catherine bit her lip. "I might have. To be completely honest, I can't remember. I'm so sorry."

"Why? You've done nothing wrong." Greg tried to put a comforting hand on Catherine's arm, but accidentally knocked an apple off a pile at a stall instead. It tumbled a short way across the cobblestones, coming to a rest at the base of the obelisk. Greg hurried over to pick it up, and in doing so, found himself facing the inscription on the base. It began:

EDIFICATO AD GLORIAM CONSTANTINO II
IMPERATORE MAGNO . . .

Greg caught his breath. While he couldn't read Latin, he didn't need to, to recognize one word. "Constantine," he repeated.

"Is something wrong?" Catherine asked him.

"No," Greg said. Then he rushed back to the apple seller. "Was this city ruled by Emperor Constantine?" he asked.

"All three of them," the seller replied proudly. "Constantine the First came here from Rome. His son was born here. And *his* son, Constantine the Usurper, made Arles the capital of his empire."

"Did any of them build a white city near here?"

The seller looked at Greg curiously. "I've never heard of anything like that. Why would they build another city when they had Arles? They made this the finest city in the Roman Empire. They built the bridges, the baths, the theater, the Arena . . . It was even more beautiful than it is now, with everything covered in marble brought all the way from the Alps."

"Everything was covered in marble?" Greg repeated. "What happened to it all?"

"People stole it," the seller said sadly. "They took it to

build other things with, the fools. Can you imagine what that Arena would have looked like a thousand years ago?"

"Yes," Greg said. He could imagine what the entire city would have looked like. His heart was now pounding in his chest, due to his excitement. He spun around the market square, taking everything in, envisioning the city as it had once been. At the far end, he spotted Aramis and Milady exiting a building.

"Are you gonna pay for that apple?" the seller asked.

Greg slapped a silver coin in the man's hand. "Thank you!" He grabbed Catherine's arm and quickly led her across the square.

"What's gotten into you?" she asked.

"This city used to be covered in marble." Greg almost felt like laughing as he said it.

"So?"

"Marble is *white*." Greg caught up to Aramis and Milady. Despite his suspicions about Milady, he couldn't control his excitement. "Aramis! I've just discovered something wonderful."

"What is it?" his friend asked.

"You know the White City of Emperor Constantine we were looking for? Well, we're standing right in the middle of it."

FIFTEEN

THE CLOISTER OF ST. TROPHIMUS WAS THE LARGEST MONastery in Arles. Founded over a thousand years earlier, it sat directly between the market plaza and the Roman theater. It was a peaceful oasis in the middle of the bustling city, centered around a central courtyard with beautiful gardens and a burbling fountain.

And, as Aramis had hoped, it had a library.

The library was quite large, almost the same size as the monastery's church, and filled with bookshelves. A dozen monks were hunched over desks, translating ancient texts.

Save for the scratches of their quill pens on parchment, it was deathly quiet.

A young monk named Brother Timothy had greeted the boys at the cloister door. Timothy had been excited to learn Aramis was a cleric from Notre Dame who had come such a long way to visit their cloister—and had eagerly agreed to show them the library, with one caveat: The girls were not allowed inside.

Greg had been pleased to hear this—he'd been scheming to ditch Milady somehow. Milady herself had been indignant, but she had ultimately capitulated and stayed with Catherine in the garden.

"What is it that you have traveled so far to find?" Brother Timothy asked now, his voice barely a whisper.

"A magic stone," Aramis replied. "According to our records at Notre Dame, this city was the last place it was ever seen."

Timothy gave him a wary glance. "We are men of God, my brother. We do not deal in sorcery."

Aramis nodded. "Of course. I'm well aware of that. But you also record history. I know what I speak of sounds impossible, but I can assure you that the Devil's Stone exists."

Greg heard a sharp gasp at the mention of the Devil's Stone. On the far side of the library, an elderly monk had lifted his head from his work. The surprise in his eyes was visible from across the room.

Aramis made a beeline for him. Greg and Timothy followed. Greg caught a glimpse of the page of text the old man was working on; it didn't look like any book he had ever seen. The writing was beautiful, ornate calligraphy and the borders of each page were filled with elaborate illustrations. "This is Brother Leo," Timothy said. "He is the finest artist we have here."

"I assume, from your reaction, that you know of the Devil's Stone?" Aramis asked eagerly.

"I do, although I have not thought of it in a long, long time." Leo's voice was tired and raspy. "I translated the tale of it from Latin when I was as young as Brother Timothy. At first, I considered it a waste of time; the story was too fantastical to take seriously. But Brother Francis, the head of St. Trophimus at the time, insisted that it was of great importance."

"Is your translation still here?" Greg asked.

Leo nodded, waved Timothy to his side, and instructed him where to find the text. Timothy hurried off into the warren of bookshelves to find it.

"Do you recall much of the story?" Aramis asked.

Brother Leo's eyes sparkled. "Quite a lot. It was one of the more interesting works I've ever done here. How much do the two of you know of the stone?"

"We know it can make men immortal—and it can allow travel through time," Greg replied.

Brother Leo shook his head and chuckled. "That's true,

I suppose. But I think you boys misunderstand the true power of the stone: When one holds it, it will make one's greatest desire come true."

"There are no limits to its power?" Aramis questioned.

"Well, I suppose there must be some," Leo admitted. "But not many. That's why the stone was regarded as being so dangerous. Humans are ill equipped to rein in their desires when given so much power. Those who held the stone generally tried to conquer their fellow men, rather than helping them. I assume you've heard of Alexander the Great. Julius Caesar. Caligula. Nero . . ."

"They all had the stone?" Greg asked.

"So the legend goes," Leo replied. "And when men weren't doing bad things with the stone, they were doing even worse things to obtain it. Battles were fought for it. Rivers of blood were spilled. Finally, after the reign of Constantine the Third, a few wise men in this city decided mankind was unfit to have the stone. So they destroyed it. They broke the stone in two and had the halves taken to the farthest ends of the Empire."

"Where?" Greg asked.

Brother Leo laughed. "There wouldn't be much point to hiding the pieces of the stone if everyone knew where they were hidden."

Greg frowned, feeling foolish. "I understand that," he said. "But we aren't seeking the stone for the same reasons others have."

"That's what everyone who comes looking for it says," Leo replied.

Greg started to press his point, but Aramis laid a hand on his arm, signaling him to back down, then tried a different tactic. "Surely, there must be more to the story of the stone, Brother?"

Leo nodded. "Yes, but the details have grown hazy in my mind. You'll have to consult the text for the rest. . . . Ah! Here comes Brother Timothy now."

To Leo's surprise, however, Timothy emerged from the bookshelves empty-handed, a look of grave concern on his face. "This text," the young monk said. "It's not there."

"It must have been misplaced," Leo said. "Someone removed it and didn't return it properly."

"Well, it wasn't one of our brothers," Timothy said. "I'm the librarian. Anyone who requires anything from here comes to me first. If that text was moved, it was done without permission."

Greg was suddenly struck by a chilling thought. "Do you ever have travelers stay here?"

"Yes," Timothy replied. "The cloister offers a place to rest for all who are weary. Why?"

"By any chance, did you offer rooms to two men around two months ago?" Greg asked. "They would have looked quite similar, almost like twins, but one was somewhat older than the other and was missing a hand."

Timothy's eyes went wide. "How on earth did you know . . . ?"

"Because we're hunting those men," Greg replied. "They're looking for the Devil's Stone. And I'd bet anything that they stole the text."

A ripple of shock went through the room. Every monk looked up from his desk.

Aramis grew uneasy with all the attention. "Could you excuse us?" he asked. "I need to talk to my colleague here in private." He dragged him into a corner and whispered to him. "How'd you know Dinicoeur and Richelieu had been here?"

"Because Dinicoeur found the stone once before," Greg explained. "And now I think I know how: the same way you did. He found the reference to the White City of Constantine at Notre Dame, then came here and found the text, which helped him track down both halves of the stone."

"So why return for the text again?" Aramis asked. "He already knows where the pieces of the stone are."

"True, but he doesn't want *us* to know. Or anyone else."

"Of course! I should have figured that out myself." Aramis sighed sadly. "Without that text, we've hit a dead end. The only one who knows how to find the Devil's Stone is Dinicoeur."

"Maybe not," Greg said. "Catherine might know a bit more than she realizes."

"Like what?"

"There's a chance one half of the stone might be back in Paris."

"Paris?" Aramis gasped. "Then why didn't Dinicoeur get it already?"

"I was wondering that myself," Greg said. "Maybe Catherine's wrong. Brother Leo said the Romans hid the halves of the stone at the farthest ends of the Roman Empire."

"A thousand years ago, Spain and Paris *would* have been the farthest ends of the Roman Empire," Aramis told him. "Catherine may be right. It's Dinicoeur's route that doesn't make sense. If only we had that text . . ."

There was a sudden commotion from the hall outside the library. The doors burst open and Porthos and Athos stormed in, with Milady and Catherine in their wake. "There you are!" Porthos's booming voice was like a bomb in the quiet library. "We've found out something important: There are no horses for sale in Arles."

"What?" Aramis asked. "How can that be? The town is surrounded by farms."

"Well, there *were* some horses for sale," Athos elaborated. "Quite a lot, we understand—but two days ago, some men bought them all."

Greg felt the hairs on the back of his neck prick up, as though something was very wrong. "Exactly how many horses are we talking about here?"

"The last merchant we talked to had sold half a dozen,"

Porthos replied. "The merchant before that had sold eight—and the one before that had sold ten."

"All to the same group of men?" Greg asked.

Athos nodded. "Plus, they cleaned out the market. Every vegetable, fruit, chicken, fish, and pig. Apparently, this city was empty yesterday. Everyone had to go back to their farms to get more food."

"Where'd they go with it all?" Greg asked.

Porthos pointed out the window toward the pontoon bridge. "That way."

Greg swallowed. Arles sat on the eastern side of the river. Across the bridge was the way to Spain. "Were the men who bought everything Spanish?"

"I asked that very question myself," Athos said. "No one could say for sure—although they'd never seen these men here before."

"There's only one reason I can think of that anyone could possibly need that much food," Greg said. "They're feeding an army."

Catherine gave a gasp of worry. Greg noticed she'd gone pale. But then he wondered if he'd done the same. Although the prospect of an invasion had been raised before, he'd figured that the most Dinicoeur could muster would be a small force, not an entire army.

"Yes, an army," Porthos said gravely. "A big one. And if they're stocking up on food from here, then they're probably not far away."

SIXTEEN

"WE NEED TO SEND A PIGEON TO PARIS," MILADY SAID.
"And we need to do it at once."

The Musketeers and Catherine raced after her as she
stormed through the city, heading for the boat, where
they'd left the birds.

"Now wait," Athos said. "Let's not be hasty. So far, it's
only a guess that Dominic has an army."

"Oh, let's not go through *this* again," Milady snapped.
"We know Dominic is allied with Spain. We know that a
group of people who appear to be from Spain are fielding

an army close by. And we know from the map that Dominic has learned the location of every secret entrance into Paris. How much more evidence do you need? Would you like him to conquer the city before your eyes?"

"No," Athos said. "But we have only five pigeons. We don't want to make a mistake. We're assuming that Dominic is connected to this army, but we have no real proof. I think we ought to do a little more reconnaissance before we sound the alarm."

Greg noticed Milady and Aramis share a glance. Something unspoken passed between them.

"I think Milady's right," Aramis said. "There's no time to waste. If Dominic has truly amassed an army and is headed for Paris, then we need to alert our own army to begin preparing as quickly as possible."

"And what if we're wrong?" Athos demanded.

"Then we send another pigeon," Aramis said. "We have four more."

Athos began to protest, but before he could, Porthos asked, "Can you conceive of any other explanation for the evidence we've found besides Dominic fielding an army?"

Athos bit his lip. "No," he admitted. "But that doesn't mean there *isn't* another explanation."

"True, but I still side with Aramis," Porthos said. "Better to send the alert now. How about you, D'Artagnan?"

Greg hesitated. He didn't want to upset Athos, but the others' arguments all made sense. Greg wondered if, perhaps, Athos was only sticking to his guns because sending the pigeon had been Milady's idea in the first place. "I think we should send the bird," he said finally.

They reached the boat. The birds were right where they'd left them, chirping happily in their cages.

Aramis wrote the note to the king on a small scrap of parchment:

> *Dominic Richelieu has amassed an army of Spaniards. They are currently near Arles en route to Paris. Do not trust the city walls to repel them. Dominic knows secret routes into the city. The army must be confronted before it reaches Paris. We will send more information when we have it.*

He signed the note, then tied it tightly to the leg of one of the pigeons with a bit of twine.

The pigeon fluttered its wings as Aramis lifted it from the cage, excited to fly after weeks in captivity. It took to the air immediately, circled their heads twice to get its bearings—and then made a beeline for Paris.

The sun was beginning to set. Without horses, there was no point in trying to leave the city so late in the day. So everyone returned to Saint Trophimus.

While the monks were still stunned by the theft of their text, they graciously agreed to house the travelers in the spare rooms—and provided them all with food and clean pallets of hay to sleep on. Immediately after dinner, the exhausted boys retired to one room, the girls to the other. Though Porthos complained about the hay smelling too "horsey," he was asleep moments after lying down. Aramis and Athos didn't take much longer. However, Greg couldn't sleep.

There were so many perplexing questions. Greg had assumed all along that Dinicoeur had gone to Spain to retrieve the stone, not an army. So why had Philip III given him one? How did the Devil's Stone factor into all of this? Did Dinicoeur have half of it already? What had he meant when he said that the other half was under the king's nose? Even with all those questions tumbling through his mind, Greg knew something else was keeping him awake: Catherine. Though he knew it was important that he get some rest, he didn't *want* to sleep. Instead, he wanted to sneak into the next room to see if Catherine was still awake as well.

Something creaked in the hall outside. Athos immediately snapped awake at the sound, and within a second, he was on his feet, sword in hand, rushing to the door. He moved so quickly, he didn't even notice Greg was awake. The swordsman slipped out into the hall—and there was a sudden gasp of fear.

"Athos! You almost scared me to death!" It was Milady. She was whispering, but in the quiet monastery, the sound easily carried to Greg's ears.

Greg glanced at Porthos and Aramis. Both were still snoring soundly.

"I didn't mean to. I was merely on the alert for danger," Athos hissed to Milady. "We are facing a treacherous enemy, you know. Why are you even sneaking about in the middle of the night?"

"I had to go to the bathroom," Milady replied.

"Did you really, now?" Athos asked suspiciously.

"Yes, really," Milady said coldly.

"And why were you creeping past our door?"

"Because it's on the way back from the bathroom. Why are you always so suspicious of me?"

"I'm not suspicious of you," Athos said, as though offended.

"Of course you are," Milady retorted. "I can't do or say a thing without you narrowing your eyes at me. You don't trust me at all, do you?"

There was a pause, as though Athos wasn't quite sure what to say. Then he asked, "Well, why should I trust you?"

"Oh, I don't know," Milady replied. "Perhaps because I've done nothing but help you. The very first day we met, I could have handed you over to Valois, but instead I introduced you to the king. If I hadn't done that, you'd probably be rotting in prison instead of parading around as a Musketeer. And since then, I've helped you plenty of times. I am the one who informed the king of your brave exploits rescuing D'Artagnan's parents. And I risked life and limb to join you on this mission."

"All right," Athos admitted. "I admit, I do owe you much."

"Then why do you dislike me so?" Milady asked.

"I don't . . ." Athos said.

"You do," Milady responded.

"How would *you* know what I think?" Athos shot back. "You barely speak to me! You spend all your time with Aramis!"

There was a stunned silence—and then, to Greg's surprise, Milady began to laugh. "Is *that* what this is all about? You're jealous!"

"I am not!" Athos protested.

"Well, there's no need for that," Milady giggled. "I don't like Aramis."

"You don't?" Now there was distinctly hope in Athos's voice.

"Well, I do," Milady admitted. "But not romantically. He's just . . . a friend. But you, I sense you have feelings for me. That's . . . good."

There was another pause. When Athos spoke again, his voice was tinged with disbelief. "You mean . . . you have feelings for me, too?"

"Yes," Milady admitted.

Greg glanced toward Aramis, worried that he'd overheard this, too, but the scribe was still sleeping peacefully.

"This is wonderful!" Athos cried. In his excitement, his voice echoed through the hall.

"Shhh," Milady warned. "I agree with you and yet . . . We have a mission of great importance to carry out—and that requires we work as a team. We can't allow emotions to get in the way. We both know Aramis has feelings for me, too. What if he knew about us? He is not as strong as you, I fear. And we can't have jealousy tearing us apart."

"No," Athos agreed. "You're right."

"And then, there is also my honor to think about. There are many who already question the propriety of a girl such as myself traveling in the company of four men."

"I shall do whatever it takes to protect your honor," Athos said.

"Then we must return to our rooms before anyone notices we're missing," Milady told him.

"They won't," Athos said. "They're all sound asleep."

"And what if they wake, just as you did? Think of my honor, Athos."

"I shall think of it all night, Milady."

Greg heard the two of them returning to their rooms. He closed his eyes and pretended to be asleep. Athos slipped back through the door, humming softly to himself, unable to control his joy.

Greg, however, felt himself consumed by anxiety. He suspected that Milady had lied about her feelings for Athos; it was the best way to win the swordsman's loyalty. Aramis was already blind to her suspicious behavior. Now there would be no convincing Athos that Milady was up to no good—if Greg could even figure out what Milady's intentions were.

Perhaps even worse was that Milady had set Athos and Aramis on a collision course. Both were smitten with her and believed she felt the same way in return. The team was barely holding together as it was—and Greg feared that Milady was the perfect spark to blow everything apart.

SEVENTEEN

"D'ARTAGNAN, WAKE UP!"

Greg pried his eyes open and found Porthos looming over him. His fellow Musketeers were already dressed. Sunlight streamed through the window.

Greg sat up, groggy. It felt as though he had only just managed to fall asleep. "What's going on?"

"We have a lead on some horses," Aramis told him. "But we must act quickly. Apparently, the seller has a rival offer."

The Spaniards, thought Greg. Wide awake now, he sprang

to his feet and quickly pulled his clothes on. "How'd this come about?"

"A man came to the monastery early this morning, looking for us," Athos explained. "He said he'd heard we were in the market for some horses and that he'd prefer to sell them to representatives of the king than foreigners."

"A load of malarkey if you ask me," Porthos groused. "He's just telling us that so he can drive up the price. . . ."

"How do you know that?" Aramis asked.

"Because it's exactly what *I'd* do if I were in his shoes," Porthos replied.

"Anyhow," Athos went on, "we need to move quickly. And not just to get the horses. Time is of the essence."

Greg fumbled his boots on, cinched his belt, grabbed his sword and hat, and followed the others out the door. Milady and Catherine were already waiting for them in the hall, fully dressed. Both looked beautifully put together, as though they had spent an hour getting ready.

"It's about time," Milady told them.

"Don't blame us," Porthos said. "Blame D'Artagnan. Waking him was like trying to rouse a stone."

Catherine laughed at this, then gave Greg a shy smile.

Greg focused on Milady and Athos, however. They betrayed nothing of the previous night's encounter. In fact, they hid their emotions so well, Greg almost wondered if he'd dreamed the entire conversation.

"Where are these horses?" Greg asked.

"The Arena," Aramis replied, "only a few blocks from here."

Greg could see the Arena, looming above, from the moment he walked out the door. The sun was still low in the sky, but Arles was already bustling. The street was full of farmers streaming into the main plaza to set up for the market. The Musketeers were the only ones headed in the opposite direction.

As Greg dodged an oxcart laden with vegetables, he nearly stumbled over a curb. To his surprise, there was an actual sewer grating in it, a crosshatch of metal that looked as modern as the ones he'd seen in Queens. But there was something unusual about it besides the fact that it was in 1615 Arles. Cold air blew out of it with a moan, as though coming from far below.

"Is that the sewer?" Greg asked.

"No," Aramis replied, looking down. "It's an air vent for the cryptoporticus."

Everyone looked at him with confusion.

"Long ago, there used to be a Roman forum here," Aramis explained. "Many of the buildings in it were quite large. The cryptoporticus was a series of arched tunnels designed to support their weight."

"What happened to the buildings?" Athos asked.

"We're probably walking over their remains," Aramis said. "Parts of this city have been knocked down twenty times over. And each time the inhabitants rebuilt, they did it right on top of the ruins."

The Musketeers emerged into a wide plaza in front of the Arena. The horse trader stood in the shadow of one of the stadiums' arches, glancing up and down the street furtively. "Come, come!" He waved the Musketeers toward him urgently. "Before anyone sees you!"

The Musketeers and the girls did as ordered, ducking under the arch as well.

"Why the secrecy?" Athos asked. "These are *your* horses to sell, right?"

"Yes, they're mine." The trader sounded offended. "But I heard the Spaniards were sniffing around town again this morning." Quickly, he led them deeper into the Arena.

The building was a testament to the versatility of the archway. Arches were everywhere. The round outer wall of the Arena was two tiers of massive arches, one on top of the other. Inside, every passage was a series of arches. One passage ringed the entire building, like the tire on a wheel, while others headed from it toward the center, like spokes. The Musketeers headed down one of these spokes now, passing under the tiers of seats. To the sides, in the darkness, there were wooden pens, from inside which Greg heard the snorting and shuffling of large animals.

"Are those the horses?" he asked.

"No," the trader replied. "Those are the bulls."

"Bulls?" Catherine asked.

"Yes." The trader grinned. "We may not have the

elaborate gladiator competitions that the Romans did, but we still hold battles here."

"You mean bullfights?" Greg asked.

"Why else would we have bulls?" the trader shot back.

From the blank looks on the others' faces, Greg realized he was the only one who even knew what a bullfight *was*. He was surprised to hear of them taking place here himself; he'd always associated them with Spain. But perhaps the culture here, this far south, was more Spanish than he'd realized.

He peered closer into one of the pens as he passed. A pair of angry eyes met his. The bull bellowed at him and slammed its horns into the side of the pen, making Greg jump.

The trader laughed. "I wouldn't get too close to them without a few years of training," he cautioned. "The bulls of Arles are renowned for their nasty tempers."

They reached the end of the passage. The trader unlatched a thick wooden gate and slid it open, allowing them all into the center of the Arena.

Greg was shocked; inside, it looked almost exactly like a modern-day stadium. The center was a large, wide oval, ringed by a wooden fence that was ten feet high and surrounded by several tiers of stone seats. The size was astonishing: It appeared large enough to hold the entire population of Arles as well as most of the surrounding countryside.

"Where are the horses?" Aramis asked.

Greg turned back to the trader, just in time to see the man slam the wooden gate shut behind them. He heard the latch being thrown on the other side, locking them in the center of the Arena.

They were trapped out in the open. There wasn't a single place to hide.

And then the arrows started flying.

EIGHTEEN

THE FIRST ARROW WHISTLED THROUGH THE AIR AND embedded itself in the gate mere inches from Greg's head.

Two more plugged the ground at the girls' feet.

The fourth struck Aramis in the shoulder.

"Ambush!" Greg yelled, just as Aramis screamed in pain.

"Run!" Athos ordered them. "Anywhere you can go! Just keep moving so they can't get a bead on you!"

Everyone did as he ordered. It was chaos. More arrows whistled past them from all directions.

Greg chanced a look up into the stands, where the arrows

were coming from. The attackers weren't even trying to hide themselves. They had no need to; there was nothing the Musketeers could do to them from this distance. The three Spanish assassins who had attacked them outside Paris had found them again. Each stood in a different section of the bleachers, with full quivers, firing arrows with abandon.

And there, along with them, was Valois. He was standing in the shadows, overseeing the attack. A sadistic smile was spread across his face.

"D'Artagnan! Come!" Athos grabbed his arm and dragged him toward the fence. "You're the best climber. I'm sending you over!"

There wasn't any time to argue—or to ask what Athos's plan was. Athos reached the fence ahead of Greg and laced his fingers together. Greg stepped into his hands and Athos lifted with all his might, launching Greg into the air. Greg caught the top of the fence, kicked at it with his feet, desperately trying to find purchase . . .

An arrow thwacked into the wood an inch from his leg.

Greg set his foot on the shaft and vaulted over the fence. He tumbled into the mud on the other side, safely out of firing range—for now.

He heard the whoosh of an arrow on the opposite side of the fence, followed by the sick, wet sound of it hitting flesh, coupled with a cry of pain from Athos.

Greg turned his attention to the fence. There was a

sliding gate close by, leading back into the center of the Arena. Greg ran over and hacked at the bolt with his sword, trying to cleave it from the fence. The wood around it splintered, weakening, but didn't give.

Something snorted behind Greg. He spun around. The huge bull he'd seen before glowered at him from the shadows. Greg was in its pen. It pawed the ground, preparing to charge, and aimed its massive horns at Greg.

Just when my day was going so well, Greg thought. His back was to the gate. There was no place for him to go. . . .

Except up. As the bull bellowed and charged, Greg jammed his sword into the wood behind him, then stepped on it and lunged for the top of the gate. His fingers caught it and he pulled himself up.

The bull slammed into the gate just beneath his feet. The weakened bolt ripped from the fence and the gate swung open. The bull's momentum carried it right out into the center of the ring.

Greg's friends were scattered around the floor. Porthos was propping up Athos, who had been hit in the thigh. Aramis was still staggering about with the shaft of an arrow protruding from his shoulder. Thankfully, neither of the girls nor Porthos had been hit yet.

"Quickly!" Greg shouted. "This way!"

Relieved at an escape route—yet terrified of the bull— the others raced for the open gate. But the Spaniards all turned their attention that way as well.

In the tier above him, Greg saw one of the Spaniards racing down toward the gate, hoping to cut off everyone's escape. Greg dropped to the ground, wrenched his sword free, then ducked back into the bull's holding pen.

Behind him, Aramis, Catherine, and Milady were almost through the gate, though Porthos and Athos were moving slower.

In the center of the ring, the bull turned back toward its pen, bellowed, and charged. It was so big, its hooves made the ground tremble.

There was a ladder built into the wall of the bullpen, heading up through a small gap between the fence and the stone tiers of seats. Greg scrambled up through it and leaped into the seats, only to find the Spaniard bearing down upon him.

Focus, he told himself. *Stay in the moment. He'll indicate what he's about to do.*

Aramis, Catherine, and Milady came through the gate below. Porthos and Athos were almost there, but the bull was bearing down on them.

The Spaniard whipped out his sword as he hurtled down the steps, then brought it back above his head, as though he intended to cleave Greg in two.

Greg ducked down and came in low with his own sword, catching the Spaniard just below the knee, using his attacker's own momentum against him. The Spaniard stumbled and sailed over the edge of the tier, landing in the gateway right after Porthos and Athos ran through.

The bull slammed into him a second later. The Spaniard screamed as the angry beast tossed him about like a rag doll.

While the bull was distracted, Greg helped the others up the ladder and into the seats. More arrows sailed toward them, clanking off the stone.

Greg caught a glimpse of Valois across the Arena. He was no longer merely watching the event. He was on his feet now, rushing into battle, a frown creasing his face.

A nearby arch led out of the seating area. Greg herded Aramis and the girls toward it, then stayed behind to help Athos up the ladder. The swordsman was bleeding profusely from his wound. He couldn't place any weight on his wounded leg, and he was beginning to grow pale.

"Are you all right?" Greg asked him.

"I'll be fine." Athos smiled gamely. "It's just a scratch."

"My uncle's beans it's just a scratch," Porthos huffed. "We need to get him to safety, fast."

He and Greg slung Athos between their shoulders and raced up the aisle and through the arch. It led to a stairwell. The boys started down it, though they'd only made it a few steps when they heard one of the girls scream.

"Go help them!" Porthos said. "I'll take care of Athos!"

Greg started to protest, wondering what *he* could do, but Porthos cut him off.

"You're the best swordsman of us, after Athos," Porthos

told him. "I'd only get myself killed."

Greg hesitated, then ran down, wondering if that could possibly be true. Porthos's words filled him with confidence, but it was tinged with doubt. There was no time to think, however. The others were in trouble, and he was the only one who could help.

Greg raced into the maze of archways that supported the Arena. Ahead, he caught a glimpse of one of the Spaniards pursuing Catherine out of the stadium and into the city. There was no sign of Aramis or Milady, but Greg assumed they must be ahead of Catherine and took up the chase.

He charged out of the Arena, into the ruins of the ancient Roman theater across the plaza, coming upon the Spaniard just as he was about to pounce on Catherine.

"Leave her alone!" Greg shouted, slamming into the assassin. They smashed through an ancient railing and tumbled into an opening in the ground beyond it. The earth dropped out from under them and they plunged into darkness.

They fell down an ancient stone staircase. Greg was battered repeatedly, landing on the hard steps—or the Spaniard—again and again until they both came to a stop with a painful thud. Greg scrambled to his feet, completely disoriented for a few moments, until he realized that he and the Spaniard had fallen down into the subterranean level beneath the city. They were in the cryptoporticus.

It was surprisingly large, the size of a subway tunnel, and almost entirely dark.

Greg had lost his sword during the long tumble down the stairs, but the Spaniard still had his. It gleamed as it sliced through the air.

Greg quickly dodged and rolled. The sword whooshed past him. He scrambled away, searching for anything to defend himself, but the crypt was barren as could be.

The Spaniard attacked again. Greg ducked away once more. His entire body ached with exhaustion, and yet he needed to run. He skirted another attack and headed deeper into the shadows.

Only to find himself in a dead end.

Greg whirled back toward the assassin. Aware Greg was trapped and unarmed, the Spaniard laughed, and the sound echoed ominously through the crypt. He raised his sword a final time. . . .

And then he gave a startled gasp of pain.

The tip of Greg's sword was now protruding from his chest. The Spaniard looked down and stared at it, as surprised to see it as Greg was.

Then he toppled forward, face-first, revealing the rest of the sword sticking out of his back.

Catherine stood behind him, stunned by what she'd done. "Oh my," she gasped. "I . . . I killed him."

Before Greg knew it, he was hugging her tightly. "If you hadn't, he'd have killed me."

Catherine clutched him tightly as well, and then began to cry onto his shoulder, overwhelmed by everything that had happened. Greg wasn't sure what to do. He stood there in the dark, wishing he could think of something reassuring to say.

As he did, his eyes adjusted to the darkness and he could now see that the cryptoporticus was partly built from pieces of other, even older buildings. Many had writing on them—at least two appeared to be ancient tombstones, now tilted on their sides—almost all of it Latin. But one was different. It was an ancient stone, extremely worn with age, decorated with the type of writing from an era that predated the Romans.

Greg sucked in a breath. To his astonishment, several of the characters looked familiar. They matched the ones on Richelieu's map.

"It's Greek," he said, before he could stop himself.

Catherine pulled back from him, red eyed and sniffling. "What is?"

Greg pointed to the stone nearby. "The inscription on Richelieu's map," he explained. "It's not a code. It's ancient Greek, like this."

Catherine looked closely, then broke into laughter.

"What's so funny?" Greg asked.

"You," she said. "Here we are, in a crypt, after men have just tried to kill us . . . and instead of dealing with that, you're off solving mysteries."

"I'm sorry," Greg said. "I just happened to notice it and . . ."

"No need to apologize," Catherine said. "I meant it as a compliment."

It occurred to Greg that his arms were still around her. He suddenly found himself looking into her eyes, overwhelmed by a tumult of emotions. She stared back, appearing equally unsure what to do.

"D'Artagnan!" Porthos's voice echoed down the stairs. "Are you down there? Are you all right?"

Greg and Catherine pulled apart awkwardly, the moment between them over. "Yes!" Greg called back. "And I'm with Catherine and one of the Spaniards—although he won't be causing us trouble anymore."

"You mean Milady isn't down there with you?" There was now concern in Porthos's voice.

"No!" Catherine raced for the stairs. "We thought she was with Aramis!"

"He thought she was with you!" Porthos yelled back.

Greg tugged his sword out of the Spaniard's back. There was blood all over the shaft. Queasily, he wiped it off on the dead man's clothes, then ran from the crypto-porticus.

He found the other Musketeers and Catherine gathered at the top of the stairs. Aramis and Athos were nursing their wounds, but while both were in great pain, they appeared far more concerned about Milady than themselves.

"What happened to Valois and the last assassin?" Greg asked.

"They fled," Athos said. "I didn't see where. But I'm guessing they captured Milady."

"No." Aramis shook his head. "They couldn't have. She's too clever to let that happen. She must be still hiding around here somewhere."

He was wrong, however. The Musketeers combed the area but found no trace of Milady. She was gone.

NINETEEN

THE MUSKETEERS QUICKLY RETURNED TO ST. TROPHIMUS to see if Milady might have returned there. The monks hadn't seen her, but one of them knew where to find the horse trader who had betrayed the boys. His name was Augustus, and he had a small office just off the market square.

Athos set off for it immediately, even though he was in terrible pain. He hobbled along so quickly that his fellow Musketeers had to pursue him through the streets.

"Athos, wait!" Porthos implored him. "You need to go

easy on that leg! We need to clean and dress that wound!"

"There will be time for that later!" Athos said. "As soon as this trader gets wind of what's happened, he'll most likely flee as well."

"And you'll die from blood loss," Greg argued. "Listen to reason, will you?" He looked toward Aramis—who was usually the voice of reason—for help. But Aramis had said almost nothing since Milady's disappearance. He, too, had refused to tend to his wound. He was so distraught about Milady, he barely looked up to see where he was going.

Athos, meanwhile, was consumed by rage. Despite his wounded leg, he hadn't stopped moving since the Arena. He'd merely cinched a tourniquet around his thigh and had been charging about the city, determined to track Milady down.

"What's got into him?" Porthos whispered to Greg as they reached the market plaza. "The way he got along with Milady, I'd have thought he'd be *happy* she's gone."

"You know how chivalrous Athos is," Greg said, afraid to divulge the truth. "If there's a damsel in distress, he has to save her."

Catherine was right on their heels. Her emotions seemed to be a mixture of Aramis's despair and Athos's resolve.

But Greg was wary. The more he played the ambush at the Arena over in his mind, the more convinced he was that Milady had betrayed them. He thought back to the day at the waterfall. Had Milady somehow left a message for Valois? That would explain how Valois and the assassins had found them. And now that the attack had failed, Milady had fled with Valois before being exposed as a traitor. Most likely, they had gone to regroup with Dinicoeur, Richelieu, and the army.

But there was no way Greg could tell the others that. He had no proof—and was sure Athos and Aramis wouldn't even believe him if he did.

And yet, even Greg had to admit there was still a chance he was wrong about Milady. What if she truly was innocent? Perhaps Valois and the assassins had tracked the boys down without any help and now had captured Milady. If that were the case, Greg would feel terribly guilty if anything happened to her. But there was something about this that didn't quite make sense, and he had a nagging feeling that he'd missed something important.

Once the Musketeers reached the market, it wasn't hard to locate the horse trader. They merely had to follow the smell. There was a stable on the far side of the plaza that reeked of horse manure, as if it hadn't been cleaned out in days, if not weeks. There was only a single horse in it at the time—a flea-bitten nag so starved her ribs poked through her skin—and Augustus was currently trying to sell her.

He went white with fear the moment he saw the Musketeers. "You!" he gasped, as though they'd risen from the dead. Then he ran for the door.

Athos was on him in a second. Ignoring the pain in his

leg, he charged through the stables and pounced on the trader. They smashed through the gate of an empty stall and slammed into the ground. Augustus was driven face-first into a two-day-old pile of manure.

Athos grabbed a handful of Augustus's hair, yanked his head up, and hissed in his ear. "Where did they go?"

"Who?" Augustus asked.

Athos slammed the trader's face back into the manure. "You don't want to play stupid with me," he snarled. "Four men hired you to help them kill us. Only two of them are still alive. Unless you want to be next, answer the question."

He yanked Augustus's face up again. The trader gasped for breath. "I don't know where they went . . ." he began.

Athos snapped a knife out of his boot.

"Wait!" Augustus pleaded. "Let me finish! I'm telling the truth about not knowing where they went. . . . But I do know *some* things that may be of help."

"Like what?" Athos demanded.

"They were an odd group: three Spaniards and a Frenchman. Although the Frenchman was the leader, the Spaniards didn't like him. They talked behind his back—in Spanish, so he wouldn't understand."

"But you did?" Athos asked.

"Yes. I speak Spanish," Augustus replied. "They didn't know, so they didn't realize I could understand them. They said they were glad this mission would soon be over so they could regroup with their countrymen."

"That's exactly what they said?" Porthos asked. "'Regroup with their countrymen?' Not 'Return to Spain'?"

"Yes," Augustus said. "Regroup. Like there were more of them around here. You're aware that someone has been buying up every bit of food and livestock in the countryside?"

"We've presumed there's an army nearby," Greg put in.

"That's the guess of everyone in Arles as well," Augustus agreed.

"And yet, you've all gone and supplied it," Athos snarled through clenched teeth. "Even though it has invaded our country."

"And what would *you* do if you were in our position?" Augustus asked. "If we refuse to sell to the Spaniards, they'll simply take what they want. There is no one to stop them. Paris has never done a thing for us. You are the first emissaries from the king any of us have ever seen in our lives. Louis has never sent an army here to protect us from the Spaniards. He only cares about protecting himself and his precious capital city."

Greg shared a self-conscious look with Porthos. Augustus had a point.

Athos wasn't so convinced. "The king hasn't sent an army because he has no idea this is happening. We have only just informed him of the possibility. . . ."

"Oh," Augustus said. "So the king's defense isn't that he

doesn't care about us. It's that he's ignorant."

Athos flushed red, but Greg stepped in before he could take his anger out on Augustus. "I think we've got offtrack here," Greg told the trader. "You want the king to send an army? We can make him do it. The more we know about the Spanish, the more we can help. Do you have any idea where this army might be?"

"From what I understand, most of the goods the Spanish have purchased have been delivered to the countryside west of Nîmes," Augustus said. "If there's an army, that's where it must be. And I'm guessing the assassins who came after you went to meet them there."

"Then that's where Milady is." It was the first time Aramis had spoken in more than an hour. The clue to Milady's whereabouts had injected new life into him, as though he suddenly had a glimmer of hope again. "But . . . Nîmes is north of us, isn't it?"

"Northwest," Augustus corrected. "About a day's ride."

"So . . . they're not heading toward the river?" Aramis asked. "How do they intend to get to Paris?"

"Overland, I suppose," Augustus said. "The Rhône might be the fastest route for a small force, but there's no way an entire army could travel up it. There aren't enough boats in all of France. But there's an old Roman road from Nîmes that heads north. . . ."

"To Paris?" Porthos inquired.

"I assume so," Augustus said. "Although I can't say for

sure. I don't know anyone who's ever gone the whole way there. I've only been as far as the aqueduct."

"What aqueduct?" Aramis demanded.

"The Pont du Gard," Augustus explained. "The Romans built it. It used to bring water to Nîmes, but it stopped working two hundred years ago. It still functions as a bridge, though, over the Gard River."

The Musketeers looked to one another. It seemed to Greg that they were all of one mind immediately.

"We need to go to Nîmes," Aramis said. "To observe this army and rescue Milady."

"My thoughts exactly," Porthos agreed.

"I've told you everything I know," Augustus said. "Have I absolved myself?"

"Not quite yet." Athos got back in the trader's face. "We need some horses."

"I don't have any more!" Augustus cried. "I swear it."

"But you know where to find some, I'm sure." Athos tightened his grip on Augustus's hair. "Six horses would go a very long way toward absolving your sins. Otherwise, I believe the penalty for conspiring to kill a Musketeer is death."

"Six horses," Augustus said quickly. "I think I might know someone."

Within fifteen minutes Augustus had tracked down six of the remaining horses in Arles. Athos refused to let Augustus out of his sight for an instant, lest the trader attempt to betray them again, so he and Porthos stayed with him while Aramis, Catherine, and Greg headed back to the boat to gather their gear.

"We ought to send another pigeon," Aramis said as they hurried down the dock. "To let the king know the Spaniards will be coming over the Roman road, rather than from the Rhône."

"But we don't know that for sure," Greg cautioned. "We only have four pigeons left. Perhaps we should wait until we know the army's route before wasting one."

"It's a moot point," Catherine said, pointing to their boat.

The cage that had held the pigeons had been smashed to bits. The birds—and thus, their only ability to communicate with Paris—were gone.

TWENTY

ALTHOUGH THE OTHERS WERE IN A DESPERATE HURRY TO leave the city and track down Milady, there was one more essential thing Greg needed to do before they left. While the others packed up the horses, he raced back to St. Trophimus.

Brother Timothy answered the door. "Can anyone here read Greek?" Greg demanded.

"Brother Leo can," Timothy replied.

Greg didn't even wait for Timothy to lead him to the library. He charged through the monastery and found

Brother Leo exactly where he'd last seen him, hunched over his desk.

"Begging your pardon, Brother," Greg said. "But I have something I need translated."

"I'll be with you in due time," Leo said, without looking up.

"It won't take long," Greg pleaded. "And I'm in a very big hurry. . . ."

"I'm sure you've heard that patience is a virtue," Leo chided. He dipped his quill pen in ink, then delicately shaded one of the pictures on the border with painstaking care.

"I think this will help keep the man who stole the text from you from recovering the Devil's Stone," Greg said.

Leo looked up from his work, and Greg proffered Dinicoeur's map and pointed at the letters on it. "Can you read this?"

Leo took the map and studied it. After a few seconds, Leo handed the paper back with a quizzical expression. "I can read it, though it doesn't make much sense to me. All it says is 'the crown of Minerva.' Does that mean anything to you?"

Greg frowned. He'd been hoping for much more than that. "Not really," he admitted. "I don't even know who Minerva could be."

"She was a Roman goddess," Leo offered. "The equivalent of the Greeks' Athena. Goddess of wisdom, medicine, commerce, poetry, music, and magic."

"Still doesn't help." Greg snuck a glance at his watch. It was time to get back to the others. "Sorry for wasting your time, Brother. I must get back to my friends."

"The pursuit of knowledge is never a waste of time," Leo replied, but Greg was already racing out the door.

As he ran back through the streets of Arles, he chided himself for ever thinking the translation might solve his problems. What had he expected, that Dinicoeur would have written 'The second half of the Devil's Stone is right here' on his map?

Maybe the inscription didn't even pertain to the Devil's Stone, Greg thought now. Maybe it was merely idle doodling. Maybe Dinicoeur hadn't even written it. . . .

Greg's step faltered as a thought came to him.

Milady. She had given them the map. She had only shown it to the Musketeers, not the king—and she had been the one to suggest that Dinicoeur planned to invade Paris. It must have been a diversion—a ruse. She had been manipulating them all along, pushing them closer and closer to the Spanish army. He was sure of it now.

But why? Was it merely to lure them into an ambush—or was she up to something else?

He reached the pier, where the others had the horses loaded and waiting.

"It's about time," Athos said testily.

"Don't mind him," Catherine said. "We only finished

with the horses a minute ago. Did you find out what you needed?"

"Not really," Greg said. "Does anyone know of a crown of Minerva somewhere in Paris?"

The others all shook their heads. "Doesn't mean anything to me," Porthos said.

"Me, either," Aramis admitted sadly. "Sorry."

Greg sighed. Every time he thought he was getting closer to the Devil's Stone, it seemed he ended up going backward.

"Let's go," Athos said. "We've wasted enough time here. A girl's life may hang in the balance." He sprang onto his horse.

Greg followed his friend's lead. Even if Milady wasn't in peril, Dinicoeur still had to be confronted.

As they all spurred their horses and rode out of the city, Greg realized there was nothing he could do about his hunch that Milady was working with the enemy. He was certain no one would believe him.

TWENTY-ONE

By the time the Musketeers located the Spanish army hours later, it was no longer west of Arles. It was on the move, now north of Nîmes, getting closer to Paris with each step.

And it was significantly larger than anyone had imagined.

"Good heavens," Catherine gasped. "There must be two thousand soldiers."

"At least," Porthos said, growing pale.

They all watched the army from atop a high ridgeline.

The forest here was different from that near Paris; the trees were scraggly and stunted, struggling to survive on the rocky slopes, though they still provided the Musketeers with decent cover for their reconnaissance.

The Spanish were marching on the Roman road, which wound along the floor of the narrow valley below, flanking the southern bank of the Gard River. The river, swollen from summer rains, was a raging torrent of water a quarter mile wide. Anyone who tried to pilot a boat across it would be taking their life in their hands.

The Roman road was still in surprisingly good condition, given that it had been built a thousand years earlier. The Spanish army filled it, marching eight men across in lines that stretched from one bend of the valley to the other.

Not far down the slope from the Musketeers were the remains of the ancient water-delivery system the Romans had built. A three-foot-wide cement sluice ran along the hillside, perfectly canted so that water had once flowed downhill through it for over fifty miles to Nîmes, an incredible feat of engineering. The sluice was still able to carry water; according to some local herdsmen, the problem was that the water pumps at the source had long ago fallen apart due to poor maintenance.

Greg watched the Spaniards snake along the riverbank. They were too far away for him to make out specific faces. He wished he had binoculars or a spyglass to see closer. "Can anyone make out Michel or Dominic?" he asked.

"Or Milady?" Catherine added.

Everyone shook their heads. "There's a man dressed very formally up at the front of the whole procession," Athos said. "I'd guess that's Michel or Dominic, but I can't tell for sure."

"Truth be told, we don't even know if Michel or Dominic is with this army," Aramis admitted. "That's still just a guess on our part."

"Same goes for Milady," Porthos said. "I'd expect that, if she was down there, she'd be held as a prisoner. Chained up on a horse or something. But I don't see anyone like that."

Greg looked at his fellow Musketeers and Catherine, their faces etched with grave concern. The size of the advancing force below—combined with how little they knew about their enemy—was daunting. And concern about Milady had depressed everyone else's spirits even further. "At least we've given the French army advance notice they're coming," Greg said, trying to cheer everyone up.

Everyone grew quiet. Athos and Porthos both shook their heads.

"What's wrong?" Greg asked.

Porthos looked up. "The French army is nowhere near as large nor as disciplined as this." He waved toward the Spaniards below them. "If they were to meet in the field of battle, the French would be decimated. If only there was a way to warn them. . . ."

"Well, there's not," Athos said. "Not with our pigeons gone. Save for us riding back to Paris with the news ourselves."

The others all nodded, though no one seemed pleased by this. The idea of racing all the way back to Paris again with bad news was onerous. In addition, Greg felt Aramis and Athos probably couldn't handle it; riding just this far had been difficult for them. The constant jouncing from the ride had inflamed both their wounds.

"There is one other course of action," Aramis said. "We could try to turn back the army ourselves."

Porthos wheeled on him, wide-eyed. "Are you insane?" he cried.

"We owe it to the people of France to try—" Aramis began.

"Our responsibility is to the *king*," Athos interrupted.

"And *his* responsibility is to his people," Aramis countered. "Or at least it ought to be. Augustus had a point: The crown has done nothing to protect the people of this region. If we merely run back to alert Paris, how many other towns and communities will be overtaken by this force? Even if, by some miracle, the king's army repels the Spanish, the allegiance of the French people might still be lost. And then the country will be lost as well."

"That's a perfectly valid point," Porthos said. "But you're forgetting something very important: There are only five of us and thousands of them. And two of us are injured."

"I can still wield a sword," Athos said defensively.

"Perhaps, but you can't run." Porthos pointed to Athos's wounded leg. "Or were you expecting one of us to carry you into battle?" He then turned to Aramis. "And you can barely work a sword on a good day. Now that your shoulder is hurt, you might as well just wave a surrender flag."

"I can fight," Catherine offered.

"You're a woman," Porthos said dismissively.

"So what?" Catherine asked, offended. "I saved D'Artagnan's life."

"Okay, fine," Porthos gave in. "You killed one man. Now, if you could kill two thousand, I'd welcome you onto our team. But you can't. In fact, none of us can. Not alone. Not together. If we try to fight that army, all we'll do is get ourselves killed. I can guarantee you that."

"Agreed." Athos looked directly at Aramis and said, "Any attempt to confront the Spanish alone would be idiocy. We're not doing it."

"Now listen here!" Aramis snapped. "I've had about enough of your insubordination! The king made me the leader of this team. . . ."

"Well, the king isn't exactly a genius," Athos shot back. "Making you our leader was obviously a mistake."

"Now wait," Porthos said quickly, before things could deteriorate further. "Aramis *is* a good leader, and we all know he's the smartest of us. . . ."

"Smarter than *you*, perhaps," Athos said.

Porthos flushed, insulted.

Before Greg knew it, the three of them were shouting at one another. Every grievance they'd had over the last few weeks boiled over at once. They were all so angry, they seemed to have forgotten where they were. Greg feared their voices would carry down into the valley and alert the Spanish to their presence.

Catherine obviously shared his concern. She looked at him pleadingly. "D'Artagnan, you have to do something."

Greg nodded, quickly getting to his feet. "Quiet!" he demanded. "All of you! Shut up right now!"

To his surprise, everyone did exactly what he'd told them to, and suddenly the woods were silent again, the others staring at him expectantly.

"There's far more at stake here right now than our feelings," Greg told them. "You might all hate each other at the moment, but I know you care about doing what's right. That's why you're Musketeers. Our country needs us to be a team right now, so we all need to put our differences aside and *stay* a team."

The other three Musketeers looked from one to another, as though ashamed of their behavior. Then Athos turned to Greg and asked, "What would you have us do?"

"What the king asked of us when he made us Musketeers," Greg replied. "You can think whatever you want about him, but he certainly understood our strengths when he assigned us our roles—and we should use those strengths now. Athos, you're the best fighter among us. There's no one I'd rather have protect me. Porthos, you're the best at thinking on your feet. There's no one I'd trust more to get me out of a tight spot. And Aramis, you're the brains, so if you have an idea . . . I think we'd all better listen to it."

Athos held Greg's gaze for a long time, then nodded. "Okay," he said. "You're right. Aramis, forgive my insolence. What do you have for us?"

Aramis smiled and waved the others in to gather around him. As they came forward, Catherine stepped up beside Greg and said, "I'm guessing your strength is holding this team together."

"Exactly what the king assigned him to do," Porthos said.

"Well, he's very good at it," Catherine said. And to Greg's surprise, she slipped her hand into his and gave it a squeeze.

Greg felt a flush of excitement surge through him, but there was no time to think about it. There were other things to focus on at the moment.

"I never said we should *fight* that army," Aramis told them all. "I said we should try to turn it back."

"There's a difference?" Porthos asked.

"Quite a big one," Aramis replied. "For one thing, there's significantly less chance of us ending up dead."

"But there's still a chance?" Porthos wanted to know.

Aramis paused before answering. "Yes," he admitted.

"What's your plan?" Greg asked.

Aramis pointed to the sluice below. "This runs all the way to the Pont du Gard. It's the only bridge over the Gard River. If we were to take it out, the Spanish wouldn't have any other way to cross."

"Unless they build a new bridge," Athos countered. "Or boats."

"All of which will take time," Aramis said. "It could take months to build a bridge. And as we can all see, the Gard is far too treacherous to take a boat across. Yes, the army could backtrack and try to find another route north, but that will also take a great deal of time. And time is valuable to an army. The more they waste, the less food they have to go around and the more disgruntled the forces become. Soldiers begin to defect. I can't guarantee that taking out the bridge will repel all the soldiers—but it may demoralize them. It will also buy us time to get to Paris and assemble a stronger defensive force—and it will send a message to the local people that the king is trying to protect them."

The Musketeers all looked from one to the other. Greg knew—as did the others—that Aramis had a very strong argument. Trying to take out the bridge seemed like a far better plan than simply running back to Paris—although the thought of even attempting it was extremely daunting.

"This won't be easy," Athos finally said.

"No, it won't," Aramis agreed.

"I assume we're going to need a great deal of explosives?" Porthos asked.

"Yes," Aramis said. "But I know where we can get it."

He pointed down the hill to the bottom of the valley. Toward the rear of the army procession, teams of oxen pulled carts heaped with barrels of gunpowder.

Greg's heart sank. "We have to steal it?"

"Don't worry," Aramis said with a smile. "As usual, I have a plan."

PART THREE

THE AQUEDUCT

TWENTY-TWO

As Michel Dinicoeur stormed through the army camp, word of his approach rippled ahead of him. *"El general! El general!"* the soldiers whispered, then scrambled to present themselves as he passed. Normally Dinicoeur appreciated the respect, but tonight he was in a foul mood. He blew past the soldiers without as much as a glance, homing in on his tent.

The army was camped on a wide plain on the south bank of the Gard River, two miles short of the Pont du Gard. Dinicoeur would have preferred to have made more progress before stopping for the night, but beyond this point the river valley narrowed sharply and there would have been no space to accommodate so many men.

Dinicoeur commanded over two thousand soldiers. The army camp was bigger than most cities in France. The size of it surprised even Dinicoeur himself. When he had first approached Philip III about fielding an army to overthrow Louis, Dinicoeur had expected a few hundred soldiers at most. But Philip had sparked to the idea of conquering France with even more relish than Dinicoeur had anticipated. He'd originally offered well over a thousand men, and the ranks had kept swelling as the army had progressed north. Of course, Philip had supplied three generals as well, not trusting his soldiers to be led solely by a Frenchman, but they were now dead and buried, thanks to Dinicoeur. He and he alone was in control of the largest army to invade France since the Roman times.

He reached his tent, which sat in the middle of the camp. The camp was laid out in concentric rings, with the least important soldiers on the outside and the leaders in the middle.

Two soldiers stood guard on either side of the entrance. "*Mi general!*" they said in unison, then pulled aside the tent flaps so he could enter.

The tent was quite well furnished, given the circumstances. There was a desk, a chest for clothes, and even a small bed. Demanding some luxury might have been a bit decadent, but it also commanded respect.

Valois was waiting inside. He had made himself at home, sitting at the desk and honing his sword with a whetstone, though he snapped to his feet when Dinicoeur arrived. "Michel. This is quite an army you've amassed."

"Keep your voice down, you fool!" Dinicoeur snapped. He came to Valois' side and hissed in his ear. "As far as anyone knows, I am Dominic Richelieu."

"But . . ." Valois began.

"Dominic and I decided it would be less confusing if there were only one of us here. He commanded the army for the first few weeks, while I attended to some other business in Madrid. Then I caught up to the army and we switched places. None of these idiot Spaniards has even noticed . . . as long as I've kept *this* hidden." Dinicoeur held up his right arm. He had a glove pulled over the stump where his hand had been.

"Where is Dominic now?" Valois asked.

"He is monitoring our progress from a safe distance." Though Dinicoeur didn't say it, there was another reason he wanted Richelieu separated from him. It was dangerous to be in an army. As an immortal, Dinicoeur could handle anything that came at him—but if his younger self died before they got both halves of the Devil's Stone, then Dinicoeur's existence would be negated as well.

Valois looked around at Dinicoeur's furnishings and chuckled. "This looks pretty safe to me. You're surrounded by an entire army, living better than a king. What do you have to be afraid of?"

Dinicoeur looked at Valois pointedly. "The failures of my underlings." He suddenly lashed out with his good hand and seized Valois's arm. "I am already tired of your insolence. You haven't earned the right to talk like that to me. I hear the Musketeers are still alive."

"It's not my fault!" Valois pleaded, his eyes wide in fear. "It was those so-called assassins who failed, not me!"

"Philip assured me they were his finest men," Dinicoeur said.

"Then that speaks poorly of Philip's army. I handed those boys to them on a silver platter—twice—and both times they failed to kill them."

Dinicoeur suddenly threw Valois to the floor. "Any failure of a team is a failure of its leadership," he said, seething. "They are only four boys! You had four assassins at your disposal!"

"They are not mere boys." Valois staggered back to his feet. He looked meaningfully at the spot where Dinicoeur's right hand had once been. "You learned that yourself, did you not?"

Dinicoeur stared at the stump of his arm and felt rage course through his body. "Yes, I did. That is one of the many reasons I want them dead. Now, no more excuses. Tomorrow, at first light, you will take *ten* men, you will leave this camp, and you will not return until you have the heads of all four Musketeers."

Valois nodded. "I shall do as you desire. But I must ask, are the Musketeers worth so much trouble? You have an entire army at your disposal. Soon France will fall and Philip will install you as king. What can the Musketeers possibly do to stop you?"

"I don't know," Dinicoeur admitted. "But I don't intend to give them the chance." As he spoke, he became aware of a strange sensation in his chest. It took him a moment to realize it was the half of the Devil's Stone, which he now wore as Philip had, beneath his clothes. It was pulsing softly, as though releasing energy.

Dinicoeur almost reached for it, but then caught himself before revealing the amulet to Valois. The stone was one of the many secrets he kept from Valois. No one knew about it except Dominic Richelieu . . .

And Greg Rich.

At the thought of Greg, the stone's pulsing increased slightly. Dinicoeur had felt the stone act like this only once before, when he'd faced his younger self, although this time was different. The pulse was more muted, the energy altered.

Dinicoeur couldn't explain it, but somehow, he suddenly understood what it meant. The stone, even just half of it, could sense his blood. Richelieu was his blood. Richelieu was *him*. And Greg Rich was his blood, too. A descendant four hundred years removed from him, but a descendant nonetheless.

"He's close by!" Dinicoeur said.

"Who?" Valois asked.

"Greg Rich!" Dinicoeur snarled. "And wherever he is, the other Musketeers must be with him. Find them now!"

Valois nodded. "If they are indeed close by, then they will be dead by daylight," he said, then exited the tent to assemble a new team of assassins.

TWENTY-THREE

THE SIZE OF THE PONT DU GARD WAS STARTLING.

The Musketeers had ridden ahead of the Spanish army to inspect it.

Greg had expected it to be a rather small bridge, given that it had only been designed to support water and the occasional horseback rider. Instead it was massive: sixteen stories high and nine hundred feet long, stretching between the steep, forested slopes of the valley. It was actually three bridges, each stacked atop the other. The lowest level was the largest, widest, and sturdiest, with five giant arches; it was on this level that the Roman road crossed the river. The middle level was just as tall, but longer, since the valley grew wider as it rose. The topmost level, which had carried the water, was significantly smaller, but the longest of all, with over twenty arches. The Gard River churned angrily beneath it all.

"We're going to need a big explosion to take that out," Greg said.

"Yes," Aramis agreed. "But if we set it off at just the right spot, everything will come crashing down. Right there." He pointed to the central bridge piling on the lowest level, which sat in the middle of the raging river. "We can detonate the charge on the road right above that."

"We'll have to do it from a distance," Athos cautioned. "Otherwise, we'll get blown up along with the aqueduct."

"Of course," Aramis said. "That's where *you* come in."

He then explained Athos's and Catherine's jobs to them. Athos was disappointed to learn he wouldn't be part of the force infiltrating the Spanish army, but Aramis pointed out that Athos would be of little help there with his wounded thigh.

"You're not going to be of much more help with your wounded shoulder," Athos said testily. Although everyone had agreed to work as a team, that didn't mean everyone had completely set aside their differences. "A fat lot of good that will do you in battle."

"If all goes well, there won't *be* a battle," Aramis countered.

In the end, Athos reluctantly crossed the bridge to the far side of the river with Catherine and the horses, while Greg, Aramis, and Porthos headed back down the valley toward the Spanish army on foot.

It was well into the night by the time they arrived. The tent city was surprisingly large, and Greg was daunted by the size. To make matters worse, Aramis's plan called for them to walk right into it.

Greg wasn't sure everything would work out as well as Aramis hoped. For one thing, he had no idea how they'd fit in when none of them spoke Spanish. But then, he had no other plan to suggest—and *something* had to be done. The future of human history hung in the balance. "How will these men know we're actually on their side and not just infiltrating their camp to undermine them?" Greg asked.

"Because sending three men to undermine an entire army is either stupid or insane," Porthos replied.

"Thanks," Greg said. "I feel so much better about our mission now."

"Just follow my lead," Porthos told him.

The boys shed their tunics with the fleurs-de-lis, which marked them as servants of the king, and tossed them into the woods. Then they came straight down the road toward the camp.

The Spanish sentries snapped to attention as the trio approached. Half a dozen loaded crossbows were suddenly aimed at the Musketeers.

Porthos immediately dropped his sword and raised his hands over his head. "Don't shoot!" he cried. "We want to join you! Long live Philip, king of Spain!"

Greg and Aramis raised their hands as well. "Long live Philip, king of Spain!" they echoed.

A sentry stepped forward, crossbow at the ready, looking them over suspiciously. "You are French?" he said.

"No," Porthos said, shaking his head violently. "Not anymore. Down with King Louis!" He spat on the ground.

This, the Spanish understood. They burst into laughter, then cheered Porthos's actions.

Greg and Aramis did the same, and the Spanish cheered them as well. The sentries collected their weapons and ushered them into the camp, although Greg noticed the Spanish were still keeping a careful eye on all of them.

The sentries led them through the outermost circle of tents, which seemed to be reserved for basic infantry, given that it was the most vulnerable to attack. Lots of soldiers didn't even have tents; they simply slept on the ground, huddled together for warmth. Greg caught a glimpse of one of the oxcarts laden with gunpowder. The oxen had been freed from it and grazed among the tents.

Then Greg noticed the large tent in the center of the camp. It was far away, lit from within with flickering yellow light, as though there were a fire inside. As Greg stared at it, a chill went through him. *Michel Dinicoeur is in there*, he thought, although he couldn't say how he knew for sure.

"Make way!" someone shouted. "Make way, you fools!"

Greg tensed. Although he hadn't heard that voice in months, he knew it all too well. *Valois.*

The Spanish sentries leading the boys froze. Valois came charging through the camp, followed by three of the biggest men Greg had ever seen, all armed to the teeth. Valois suddenly paused, then spun to face the sentries.

Greg, Porthos, and Aramis lowered their heads, hoping that without their Musketeers uniforms on, they would blend into the sea of other boys and men in the army. To their relief, Valois didn't notice them. He was too focused on the largest sentry.

"You," Valois said. "How well can you handle yourself in battle?"

"Very well," the sentry replied.

"Then come with us," Valois said. "I have a job for you. I am organizing a hunting party at the direct order of General Richelieu."

The sentry obediently fell in with the others, and Valois led them away without a glance back.

Greg realized he'd been holding his breath the entire time, afraid to so much as even exhale in Valois's presence.

The remaining sentries led him and the others on to a large tent that signified it belonged to someone of importance. One sentry called out a welcome, and then an imperious-looking soldier emerged. He was an older man, around forty, and he also had the fleur-de-lis on his tunic, although his was marred by a dark black scorch mark. He cast an intrigued eye at the Musketeers, conversed briefly with the sentries in Spanish, then spoke to the Musketeers in French. "Why do you wish to serve King Philip?"

"Because he couldn't possibly be more terrible than King Louis," Porthos replied. "We were soldiers in the French army, but we were treated worse than dogs. We understand King Philip is a wise man who understands the value of good warriors."

The Frenchman came closer, examining the boys in the firelight. "My name is Gérard. I served in the French army myself—under King Henry. You do not appear like warriors to me. One of you is wounded. . . ." His eyes flicked to Aramis.

"In battle, I assure you," Porthos replied. "The king sent our regiment to confront the forces of the Prince of Condé, then abandoned us. My friend here was wounded serving his king honorably, but the king did not honor us in return. That is why we stand before you now."

Gérard nodded, then shifted his gaze to Greg. "And this one?" he asked. "He barely looks as though he can lift a sword, yet alone wield it in battle."

"Then test him," Porthos said.

Greg turned to Porthos, surprised, but his fellow Musketeer just smiled confidently.

Gérard selected a sword and tossed it to Greg. No sooner had Greg caught it than the older soldier attacked. Greg parried and responded. They went back and forth, swords clanging in the firelight. Gérard was an adept swordsman, but Greg held his own, defending himself against every challenge and aggressively counterattacking.

After two minutes, Gérard suddenly stepped away, sheathed his sword, and smiled at Greg. "I stand corrected. You can fight as well as anyone under my command. Perhaps even better. What is your name, boy?"

"My friends call me D'Artagnan."

Gérard's smile grew even larger. "You're from Artagnan? No wonder you hate the king. I'm from the Roussillon, not far from you!"

And just like that, the Musketeers were welcomed into the Spanish army. Gérard ordered the sentries to return the boys' weapons. Then he ushered the boys into his tent and demanded food and water be brought for them.

While the boys ate, Gérard traded war stories with them. Porthos had to make all theirs up, but thankfully he was convincing. Aramis and Greg simply nodded in agreement to whatever he said while stuffing their faces full of food. Eventually, in the midst of spinning a tale of how they'd been betrayed by the king's army in battle at Avignon, Porthos cleverly found a way to pump Gérard for information. "There were only two men we respected in the entire army, and both of them quit in protest against the king's rule. They were named René Valois and Dominic Richelieu."

Gérard snapped up in his seat. "Valois and Richelieu? They are with us!"

The boys feigned surprise. "No!" Porthos said. "They are allied with the Spanish?"

"Even better," Gérard said. "Richelieu *commands* the Spanish. That's his tent in the center of the camp!"

Aramis couldn't help but break his silence. "Why on earth did Philip ever give Richelieu a command? Isn't his daughter due to marry Louis soon?"

Gérard laughed, as though Aramis were terribly naive. "Yes, she is. But that was merely a political move to gain access to the Netherlands through France. Philip was never pleased that he had to sacrifice Anne to Louis. So when Dominic Richelieu arrived in his court with a plan to topple France instead, Philip jumped at it. As you know, Dominic controlled the King's Guard. Thus, he knows its weaknesses—as well as those of Paris itself—very well."

"And what does Richelieu ask for in return?" Aramis asked.

"What else? Wealth and power," Gérard replied. "I suspect Philip will set him up nicely, once France falls."

"And what of Richelieu's twin brother?" Porthos asked. "Is he involved in this campaign?"

"Twin brother?" Gérard asked curiously. "I know of no such man."

Greg and the others exchanged a glance. So Michel was once again keeping himself hidden—or was posing as

Richelieu while his brother stayed hidden.

"I suppose he must not be involved," Porthos said quickly.

"But this other man you mentioned, Valois," Gérard went on. "He arrived in camp just this night. I hear he went directly to Richelieu's quarters. I haven't met him yet, but I understand he is a great warrior, extremely gifted with a bow and arrow."

"Did he arrive alone?" Aramis asked.

"No," Gérard said. "There was a Spaniard with him. They had been on some sort of mission in the countryside until now."

Aramis screwed up his face in concern. Greg knew he was worried that there had been no mention of Milady. "That's all? He was with no one else?"

Gérard shrugged. "He might have been. It's a big camp. I don't hear everything." He suddenly yawned, then grew embarrassed. "Well, it's late, and I'm sure you're even more tired than I am. I'd be honored if you would join up with my brigade."

"The honor would be ours," Porthos said humbly.

Gérard broke into a pleased smile. "Then it's settled! My officers will make room for you in their tent." He clapped his hands, and his underlings immediately sprang to attention. Gérard ordered that the boys be shown to the officers' quarters. Porthos graciously thanked him for his hospitality, they all swore allegiance to King Philip once more, and then the boys were off.

The officers' quarters weren't that impressive, merely a moderate-size tent inside which the officers slept on the ground. Most of them were already sound asleep.

"Looks wonderful," Porthos lied to the soldiers who'd led them there. "However, before turning in, I think my friends and I might take a stroll about the camp, just to make sure the defenses are up to snuff."

The soldiers, who probably couldn't have cared less whether Gérard's new recruits went to bed or not, nodded agreement and shuffled off. Suddenly, the Musketeers were alone and unguarded in the midst of the enemy camp.

Porthos grinned, pleased with himself, as usual, then led them toward the powder wagon they'd seen earlier.

Greg had been concerned that they wouldn't blend in, given their lack of uniforms, but now that he was in the camp, he discovered that almost no one had a uniform. The army was mostly a hodgepodge of men recruited from all walks of life, most of whom were serving—and sleeping—in the clothes they'd worn to enlist.

The Musketeers moved quietly through the camp, eventually reaching the powder cart. No one was guarding it—although there was a gauntlet of sleeping soldiers and sentries they'd have to pass to get it on the road.

"There's no way we'll get this out of here without being seen," Greg whispered. "It's one thing to walk into the camp and join up. But it's a whole other to waltz right out again with two tons of gunpowder."

"Have a little faith," Porthos said, unfazed. "And while you're at it, see if you can find me some horses."

"It's an oxcart," Greg protested.

"Only when you have oxen pulling it. And oxen are dreadfully slow," Porthos said. "When we go, we'll need to go fast. So find me some horses."

Greg reluctantly nodded agreement and set off into the camp with Aramis. They found two horses relatively quickly—impressive, muscular steeds tied up outside the tent of some officers. While Greg untied them, Aramis found a few handfuls of sweet grass, which the horses loved. They eagerly allowed themselves to be led away in return for more.

"Only two?" Porthos asked when they got back. "We'll need at least three to pull this cart!"

"You might have mentioned that before," Greg snapped, but he set off to find another horse while the others hitched up the cart.

It took him longer to find one this time. There were lots of other horses, but most were in such sorry shape that Greg doubted they could pull a baby carriage, let alone their share of the powder wagon. The horses that *were* in good shape were understandably well protected. The sky was already starting to turn pink with the sunrise by the time Greg happened upon a suitable horse that miraculously wasn't tied to *anything*. In fact, it appeared to have freed itself by gnawing through its tether; a short hank of rope dangled from its reins.

Greg did what Aramis had done; he found some sweet grass and offered it to the horse, which gulped it down and whinnied happily. "That's a good boy," Greg said, petting its nose. The horse nuzzled him, nice and friendly. Greg grabbed a bit more grass and the horse let him lead it away.

Greg had only taken a few steps before he realized where he was. He'd been so focused on finding a horse, he hadn't been paying attention to where he was in the camp. But now he saw that he'd come dangerously close to the center. The huge tent he'd noticed before was only twenty feet away from him.

Greg noticed a makeshift hitching post next to it. There was a chewed-off length of rope dangling from it, one that matched the piece currently in Greg's hand.

Greg gulped. He was stealing the horse of his mortal enemy.

And then, the flap of the tent flew open and Michel Dinicoeur emerged.

TWENTY-FOUR

GREG INSTANTLY KNEW IT WAS MICHEL AND NOT DOMI-
nic. The madman had a glove on the stump of his right
arm, hiding the fact that his hand was missing. He didn't
see Greg right away—although he did seem to be on the
alert. He was dressed in full military regalia—but what
really caught Greg's eye was the object that dangled from
Michel's neck: a dark piece of stone strung on a silver chain.

The Devil's Stone. Michel had already found one half.
Even without the entire stone, however, Greg could sense
that Michel was drawing strength from it. Greg didn't

know how, exactly, but he could feel it, as though Michel was surrounded by an invisible, powerful force.

Greg was about to run, leaving the horse behind, when Michel seemed to sense his presence. The madman whirled around and stared directly at Greg, fire in his eyes.

"You!" he gasped. "How . . .?"

Before Greg even knew he was doing it, he sprang onto the back of Michel's horse and snapped the reins. "Go!" he shouted.

The horse dutifully obeyed, galloping through the camp.

Michel flushed with rage. "To arms!" he yelled at the top of his voice. "The enemy is in our camp! Kill them!"

The sheer volume of his voice seemed superhuman to Greg. It echoed throughout the canyon like a lion's roar. But the soldiers, most of whom were still deep asleep, were slow to respond. Michel quickly realized this was something he'd have to handle himself. He unsheathed his sword, slashed through the rope of another horse tethered near his tent, then leaped astride it and took up the chase.

Greg thundered through the enemy camp, his heart pounding with fear. He'd gotten better at riding over the past few months, but this horse wasn't saddled, and going bareback was difficult normally, let alone at a full gallop while trying to avoid a thousand obstacles. Greg clenched the horse's flanks between his knees, clung to the reins as tightly as he could, and prayed he wouldn't fall off.

The farther he got, the more time the soldiers had to

wake and realize what was happening. Now men began pouring out of tents. Several lunged for the horse's reins, but the stallion was moving fast now. Most attackers were bowled out of the way, although one managed to cling on for a few seconds as the horse dragged him through the camp before finally getting slammed headfirst into a battering ram and collapsing, unconscious.

Greg saw the powder wagon ahead. Porthos and Aramis had apparently realized that the plan was coming undone. Aramis had found another two horses in Greg's absence, and Porthos had just finished hitching them up. They clambered onto the cart and snapped the reins. "Yah! Yah!" Porthos shouted. The horses whinnied and ran, dragging the cart and its explosive cargo along.

The cart cut a far bigger swath through the camp than Greg's single horse did—and Porthos wasn't that good a driver. The thick wooden wheels quickly flattened two tents, scattering their panicked occupants—as well as dozens of other soldiers who woke to find themselves in its path. Cages full of chickens collapsed, releasing their captives in flurries of feathers, while horses and cattle bolted in fear. Porthos swung his sword wildly, slashing at any enemy structure he could—and thus dozens of other tents collapsed in his wake.

Ahead, at the perimeter of camp, a group of soldiers were hurriedly forming a barricade. Greg recognized a few of them from earlier in the evening: the men Valois had chosen to form his hunting party. Now there were twelve men . . . and Valois stood by their side.

Valois seemed even more enraged than Michel to see the Musketeers in the camp. He glared hatefully at the boys. "Ready crossbows!" he ordered.

His men slipped their bolts into their weapons.

Porthos didn't waver for a moment. Instead, he swung his sword in the air and whooped at the top of his lungs, an act of defiance that struck fear in the hearts of those ahead. Greg and Aramis followed his lead as they bore down on the enemy.

Valois' blockade faltered. The soldiers scattered before the wagon. A few bolts flew. One managed to slice the air between Porthos and Aramis and thwack into a powder keg, but most went well wide of their targets. Greg heard a few screams behind him as unwitting Spaniards were taken down by friendly fire.

The Musketeers burst free from the camp and onto the Roman road. Once the wagon's wheels hit the evenly paved stones, it picked up speed. Greg had to spur his horse to keep up.

He chanced a look back toward the camp, which he quickly regretted. Michel Dinicoeur barreled through the ranks astride his horse, ordering his troops to arms. Behind him, dozens of soldiers—including Valois—were wrangling whatever mounts they could and joining the pursuit on horseback, while hundreds of others charged after them on foot. The entire army was now awake and bloodthirsty, two thousand men funneling onto the road in hot pursuit.

Greg heard the sound of something splitting the air and whirled around to see what looked like a ball of flame fly out of the woods along the road. He realized, to his horror, that it was a flaming arrow. It impaled a powder keg on the rear of the wagon and began to burn.

Greg glanced toward the woods, but whoever had fired the shot remained hidden. *Dominic*, Greg thought. He turned back to the wagon, knowing he had to act quickly. If the flaming arrow ignited the gunpowder, Porthos and Aramis would be toast.

The other boys realized this as well. Aramis took the reins while Porthos tried to scramble over the pile of powder kegs to the back of the wagon. However, this was too difficult while the wagon was moving. Porthos was nearly thrown off as the wagon made a sharp turn. He caught the rope that held the barrels at the last instant and clung on for his life.

Which left saving the day up to Greg. He brought his horse in as close to the wagon as he dared and slashed at the flaming arrow with his sword. He had to strain to get close enough, which would have been difficult enough with a saddle and stirrups, but was nearly impossible on an unsaddled horse, for fear of being tossed to the ground and trampled. He missed the shaft again and again, while the flame burned closer and closer to the powder in the keg.

Finally, Greg made a last-ditch effort, clinging to the horse's mane and stretching as far as he could. With a final lunge, he severed the arrow, and the flaming shaft tumbled harmlessly onto the road.

Greg heaved a sigh of relief and looked up to see the aqueduct bridge looming around the bend ahead. They were less than half a mile away. Perhaps they'd make it. . . .

There was a snort of air from behind. Greg whirled and found Michel Dinicoeur almost on top of him. He'd gained ground while Greg had been distracted by the burning arrow—and now his sword was slashing down.

Greg blocked it with his own sword. Sparks flew. Michel's horse slammed into his, which whinnied and stumbled away from the cart.

Again Michel attacked. Again Greg parried. Michel's horse slipped ahead of Greg's, cutting him off.

A path forked off the Roman road, heading up the mountain. It was stone as well, a spur of the main road, and Greg had no choice but to take it. He steered his horse onto it, leaving Michel behind for a moment, until the madman could regroup and take up the chase.

Greg's horse galloped up the slope as fast as it could go. Greg could feel it tiring beneath him. He couldn't blame it; *he* was getting exhausted as well. And still Michel came after them, his horse still going strong.

They rounded a bend and Greg realized where this

second road was taking them: to the upper level of the bridge. It appeared to be a maintenance road that accessed the second and third tiers. Greg gulped, realizing he was now heading for a narrow passageway sixteen stories above a raging river on a charging horse with a sword-wielding lunatic chasing him. And his friends were rushing to blow up that very same bridge.

Greg glanced down at the road, which was already surprisingly far below. Porthos was still dangling from the support rope, struggling to get back to his seat, while the enemy troops were gaining.

And if that wasn't bad enough, Greg noticed the last barrel on the wagon was burning. Perhaps a piece of the flaming arrow hadn't fallen off. Perhaps a spark from his sword had set it aflame. Whatever the reason, the powder keg was on fire—and his fellow Musketeers didn't know.

He screamed to them, but his voice was drowned out by the thunder of hooves and the roar of the wagon wheels. Porthos and Aramis were on their own.

TWENTY-FIVE

ATHOS SAT IN THE WOODS ON THE FAR SIDE OF THE BRIDGE, morosely tending the fire he'd built hours before. He was tired of waiting, and his wounded leg throbbed with pain. The annoyance he'd felt at being left behind had shifted to concern as the sun began to rise. His fellow Musketeers had been gone too long. He'd expected them before dawn. Something must have gone wrong.

Catherine stirred in her sleep beside him. She was curled on the ground, huddled close to the warmth of the fire. She had volunteered to remain on watch herself, but Athos wouldn't hear of it. No matter how tired he was, it simply seemed wrong for a man to sleep while a woman guarded him.

He snapped a thin branch off a tree and began to whittle it with his knife, making yet another arrow. He'd already made dozens, more than enough—he hoped. What else was there to do? He'd honed the shafts, found sharp stones to serve as arrowheads, notched the shafts, and fit the stones inside. He'd made pitch by collecting resin from the pine trees and boiling it down over the fire—and then he'd rolled the arrows in it. They were all ready to go now, dried and waiting in his quiver. . . .

The whinny of a horse echoed through the canyon. Athos jumped to his feet and instantly felt pain sizzle through his thigh. His wound wasn't healing well. He should have taken more time to treat it, and he'd been using it too much; Greg had been right about that. He needed to rest it—though there was no time for rest now.

Athos propped himself against a stump to take the weight off his leg and stared through the trees toward the bridge. Along the river beyond it, he saw two of his fellow Musketeers round the final bend of the road in a powder wagon, four horses pulling it as fast as it would go. Then, to Athos's dismay, enemy soldiers rounded the bend in pursuit. They were on horseback—and more and more kept coming. It seemed as though the entire Spanish army was after his friends.

"What's happening?" Catherine was suddenly at Athos's side, rubbing sleep from her eyes. She paled as she took in the situation. "There's only two of them. . . ."

Athos grabbed his quiver and his bow and hobbled toward the bridge as fast as he could go, trying his best to ignore the pain. "Yes. Porthos and Aramis, I think."

He heard Catherine let out a gasp of dismay. "Where's D'Artagnan?"

"I don't know," Athos said grimly. "Bring the fire!"

Catherine did as they'd rehearsed. She took a resin-soaked log and jabbed it in the campfire. It caught quickly, creating a torch. Catherine then raced through the woods after Athos.

He had already reached the Roman road, where it snaked up the mountain after it exited the bridge. Across the river, Aramis and Porthos were nearing the Pont du Gard, with the Spanish army behind them. The cacophony of hooves on the ancient stones now drowned out the river itself.

"Oh my . . ." Catherine gasped. She pointed at the hillside across the river.

Athos looked up and saw D'Artagnan on horseback, heading for the highest level of the bridge—and he was locked in a swordfight with someone else on horseback at the same time.

"That level's not nearly wide enough for the horses," Catherine said.

"No," Athos said gravely. Things weren't going to plan at all. In fact, it didn't seem things could possibly be worse.

Porthos and Aramis could hear the enemy's horses bearing down on them while their own horses were flagging. They were almost to the bridge, but it wasn't coming fast enough.

"We're not going to make it!" Aramis shouted.

"Yes, we are," Porthos said reassuringly, although he was filled with doubt himself. He focused on the far end of the bridge, hoping Athos was in place. If the plan was to work at all, Athos would need exceptional aim and timing. . . .

Aramis glanced back at his pursuers. The enemy was almost on top of them. Valois was in the lead, only a few paces behind the powder cart, grinning maniacally from his horse, as if he couldn't wait to hack the Musketeers to pieces.

Then, Aramis noticed something even more worrisome. Smoke was pouring off the back of the cart. "Porthos!" he cried. "One of the powder kegs is on fire!"

Porthos spun around and grimaced. "And just when everything was going so well," he muttered.

As they watched, the fire suddenly blossomed, tripling in size. It flamed around the hole where a cork stopper held the gunpowder in.

"The powder's starting to catch!" Aramis warned. "It's going to blow!"

The first arch of the bridge was just ahead, but they needed to get to the middle for their plan to work. "There's not enough time," Porthos admitted sadly. "There's only one thing to do." He whipped out his sword and slashed through the rope that held the kegs to the wagon.

The taut rope snapped like a broken rubber band, freeing the powder kegs. They tumbled off the back of the wagon and into the road.

Valois' eyes went wide with fear as he saw what was happening. He reined in his horse, but the rest of the army was right behind him. Their horses slammed into his, which reared to its feet and pitched Valois to the ground.

The flaming powder keg slammed into Valois—and exploded.

The other kegs went off as well, a chain reaction of explosions that decimated the front ranks of the army. The ground trembled and the stones of the Roman road soared into the air. A wave of fire rose up, scorching the earth.

Freed from the weight of all the gunpowder, the horses pulling the wagon suddenly gained speed, racing onto the lowest level of the bridge. But the concussion from the explosion lifted the wagon off its wheels and flipped it on its side. Porthos and Aramis were catapulted onto the horses, which bucked and whinnied in terror as the overturned wagon skidded wildly behind them, finally smashing into one of the arches and shattering into pieces.

Porthos and Aramis were thrown to the ground while

the horses raced onward.

The two Musketeers sat up, singed from the explosion, dazed from their falls. The bridge was still trembling from the blast, but it was well built and remained standing. The kegs had detonated too soon, leaving nothing but a wall of fire at the end of the bridge—and even that was already dying down. A few Spanish horses leaped through it, carrying their riders safely onto the bridge. And behind the flames, the Musketeers could see hundreds more soldiers amassing, ready to bear down upon them.

"We failed," Aramis gasped. "What do we do now?"

Porthos shrugged and shook his head. "The only thing left. We pray."

At the aqueduct on the top of the bridge, the sluice cut through the highest level of arches, though it was roofed with stone to protect the water supply. Where the bridge met land, the sluice continued on, carved into the rock. The service road came to a dead end here. Greg had just reached this point when the explosion occurred below.

His horse was already skittish, and now the shock wave from the blast combined with the deafening roar made it rear up in fear. Greg lost his grip on the reins and tumbled onto the sluice.

His horse retreated, slamming into Michel's, which reared as well. The madman leaped from it before he was thrown, and both horses fled back down the hillside.

Dinicoeur tumbled but came up on his feet again, sword in hand. He charged toward Greg, the fire from the explosion gleaming in his eyes.

Greg's sword had skittered farther down the bridge. Now it teetered on the edge above the abyss. Greg ran and dove for it, snatching it just before it dropped. He rolled over, blocked Michel's sword as it swung down at him, then snapped to his feet to face his enemy head-on.

The bridge was wide at the top, so there was room to maneuver, but there was no safety railing and the drop over the edge was sickeningly steep. Greg knew that, if he fell, he'd either land on the road across the first tier of arches, which would no doubt kill him on impact—or he'd plunge into the rushing river, which would most likely drown him. Neither seemed like a very good option, so Greg tried to put the fear of falling out of his mind and focus on the swordfight instead.

"Why don't you just admit defeat?" Dinicoeur snarled, slashing with his sword. "You've already lost. My army is about to annihilate your friends—and in a few weeks we will do the same to France."

"Not if I can help it," Greg said, although he could feel his strength fading. He couldn't even manage an offensive move now; Dinicoeur was coming too hard and fast. Greg was getting pushed farther and farther along the bridge. Soon he and Dinicoeur were at the dead center, where the edifice was at its highest, sixteen stories above the raging river below.

Dinicoeur laughed. "I have two thousand men at my disposal. What do you have? Nothing! You're just boys playing with swords."

"We defeated you once," Greg said.

"That was a temporary setback," Dinicoeur snapped. "And besides, you actually did me a favor. If it wasn't for you, I might have been content to stay in the king's court— but now, I will depose that foolish king and rule all of France!"

"It won't mean anything to you without the other half of the Devil's Stone," Greg told him. "Once we beat you to the other half, you won't be able to make Dominic immortal. And when we take him out, you'll die, too."

"There's just one problem with that plan," Michel taunted. "You don't know where the other half is—and I do."

"I know exactly where it is," Greg retorted. "It's back in Paris."

It was a bluff on his part—but it paid off perfectly when he saw Michel's reaction. The madman's eyes went wide in surprise, proving Greg's hunch was right. The other half of the stone *was* in Paris.

Greg took advantage of Michel's astonishment and lunged for his heart.

Dinicoeur easily sidestepped the attack. He'd seen it coming; he was a far more formidable opponent than anyone else Greg had faced—perhaps even better than Athos. And he didn't even appear to be tired. Although the Devil's Stone wasn't complete, it still seemed to be giving him strength.

"Why are you even bothering to fight?" Dinicoeur taunted. "I'm immortal, you fool! You know you can never defeat me!"

The words rang in Greg's ears. For a moment, he was daunted by them . . . but then, an idea came to him. He glanced down at the lowest tier of the bridge. The Spanish army was advancing onto it now, skirting the remnants of the fire. Then he looked back at Dinicoeur. The madman had made a mistake, Greg realized. His greatest strength was also his greatest weakness.

Greg dodged another attack—and retreated across the top of the bridge. As he'd expected, Dinicoeur came after him, seized with bloodlust, determined to kill him. As Greg ran, he spotted Athos and Catherine on the road at the far side of the river. "Athos!" Greg yelled. "Light the arrows! Light them up and shoot Dinicoeur!"

Far below, the Musketeers heard the shouts. Porthos and Aramis were running as well now, racing across the bridge before the Spanish riders could bear down on them. The army had temporarily been in disarray, as Valois and several other leaders had been blown to bits, but now it was surging forward.

On the far side of the bridge, Athos whipped an arrow

from his quiver and held it out. Catherine set the torch to it and the resin ignited. Athos quickly set it in the bow, aimed, and let it fly. Within a second, Catherine had another arrow ready. And then another. Athos shot them as fast as he could, sending bolts of fire racing through the air.

The first few missed Dinicoeur, but the fourth found him as Athos adjusted his aim. It struck the madman in the chest.

It barely pierced Dinicoeur's armor, however. Michel emitted a tiny grunt of pain, then used his sword to snap off the flaming shaft and swat it away. He had to stop running to do it, however, which finally gave Greg a good target.

Greg lunged with his sword, slashing Dinicoeur across the chest.

Dinicoeur spun around with surprising speed and punched Greg in the jaw with such strength that it sent him flying.

Greg tumbled toward the edge of the aqueduct, catching hold an instant before tumbling off the bridge. His legs dangled over the void.

Dinicoeur stormed toward him. "You have failed!" he snarled. "Failed once again in your miserable attempt to destroy me."

"I wasn't trying to destroy you," Greg said defiantly. "I was trying to get *this*."

With his free hand, he held up the half of the Devil's

Stone, displaying the links of the chain he had severed with his sword.

Dinicoeur gasped. His hand reflexively went to his neck, confirming the Devil's Stone was no longer there. For a moment, he stood there, frozen in shock. . . .

Which was all the time Athos needed.

The flaming arrow struck Dinicoeur in the shoulder. The madman roared and snapped the shaft off, but the pitch was already on his shirt, which caught fire. He screamed and spun, trying to swat out the flames.

The next arrow from Athos caught him in the leg. The one after that hit him in the arm. Dinicoeur's anger turned to panic. Even though he was immortal, he could still feel pain—and as the fire engulfed his body, it was agony. He desperately tried to peel off his blazing clothes. . . .

That was when Greg body-checked him. He caught Dinicoeur by surprise and sent him flying off the bridge.

The madman fell, screaming—and slammed into the lowest level.

He landed right in front of the advancing army. The lead riders reined in their horses in surprise.

But just as Dinicoeur had said, he couldn't be killed. Instead, he rose to his feet, screaming in fury.

Everyone gasped in horror at the flaming, raging, seemingly indestructible beast before them.

Greg shouted one of the few Spanish phrases he knew to those below him. *"El Diablo!"* The Devil.

A murmur of fear and horror rippled through the Spanish army.

"That is who you serve!" Greg shouted to them. "That is who has led you here! The Devil himself!"

"Don't listen to him!" Dinicoeur yelled. "I am no such thing!"

But his appearance meant more to the soldiers than his words did. The men were superstitious and terrified of the unknown. They turned and fled, racing back the way they had come.

"No!" Dinicoeur shouted. The fall and the pain were taking their toll on him. Even his hair was on fire now, framing his burned face in flame and making him look even more devilish than before. "I am not the enemy! They are!" He staggered toward Porthos and Aramis, his sword raised, in one desperate final attempt to lead the charge.

Porthos screamed in horror. As far as he knew, Dinicoeur truly was the Devil. And even though Aramis knew Dinicoeur was immortal, he was still terrified as well.

Then, a final arrow from Athos caught Dinicoeur in the chest. Now, from close range, it was enough to send him reeling backward. The madman toppled over the side of the bridge and plummeted into the river, which quickly whisked him away.

Greg scrambled down the hillside from the upper tier. He raced onto the Roman road to rejoin his friends. "Is everyone all right?" he asked.

"No we're not all right!" Porthos gasped. "Did you see that? Dinicoeur is the Devil! We're fighting the Devil!"

"We're not," Greg said reassuringly. "I only said that to frighten everyone else. Dinicoeur isn't the Devil—although he *is* immortal."

Porthos and Athos turned to Greg, looking shocked and betrayed. "You knew that was going to happen?" Athos asked.

"Yes," Greg admitted.

"How much else is there that you haven't told us?" Porthos asked.

Greg hesitated, unsure what to say—and in that moment, he saw something change in his friends' eyes. *They don't trust me*, he thought.

Suddenly, a woman's cry echoed through the woods. "Athos! Aramis! Help me!"

The Musketeers all stiffened at the sound, recognizing the voice at once.

"Milady!" Athos cried. Then, despite his wounded thigh, he spun and raced headlong into the forest.

TWENTY-SIX

"ATHOS! WAIT!" GREG SCRAMBLED UP THE WOODED HILL-side alongside the Pont du Gard. Ahead of him, Athos was moving with surprising speed, given his injured thigh. Greg guessed the swordsman wasn't even aware of the pain; he was too focused on helping the girl he loved.

"Look out, D'Artagnan!" Aramis sprinted past Greg, desperate to save Milady as well. The scribe didn't seem to be bothered by any of the wounds he'd suffered, either.

Only Porthos seemed to be as fatigued as Greg. He came last, lumbering through the woods, gasping for breath.

"She has to get herself into trouble *now*?" he gasped. "She couldn't wait ten minutes to let us catch our breath?"

Greg suspected the timing wasn't random at all, however. Everything seemed much too convenient; Milady just happening to show up way out here, at this moment, when the boys were exhausted and battered from battle. He called after Athos and Aramis again. "Stop! I don't think we can trust her!"

The boys each looked back his way for a second, then continued on.

Greg turned to Porthos, desperate. "Maybe you should call to them. They're not listening to me."

"Why should they?" Porthos asked harshly. "You're the one who hasn't been honest here." With that, he trudged on ahead after the others.

Greg hadn't gone far—just a bit above the point where the top tier of the aqueduct met the mountainside—but he was wiped out from the night's adventure. His legs ached and his lungs burned. He watched helplessly as his fellow Musketeers disappeared over a small rise ahead.

Behind him, on the far side of the river, he could see the last of the Spanish army retreating. It seemed he should feel some joy about this—or at least a sense of relief. After all, he and the Musketeers had managed to repel the Spanish and save France. They'd prevented Dinicoeur from altering the course of history. And he had retrieved half of the Devil's Stone, which he now clutched tightly as he staggered uphill. But still, all Greg felt was a sense of fore-boding, as if he wasn't out of this yet.

"They may not trust you, but I do." Catherine was suddenly at his side, steadying him as he struggled to climb.

Greg turned to her and saw that she meant it. "We need to stop them," he said.

"Why? What do you think she's up to?"

Before Greg could answer, there was a commotion ahead. He heard the shouts of his fellow Musketeers, the clang of swords, a scream of pain from Aramis. Catherine started to race in that direction, but Greg caught her arm. "No," he said.

"But they're in trouble."

"And if we go that way, we'll be in it with them." Greg tucked the Devil's Stone away and withdrew his sword. "We'll circle around to get the jump on them."

He had only gone a few steps, however, before Milady's voice rang through the forest. She no longer sounded as though she was in danger. Instead, her voice was almost taunting. "D'Artagnan and Catherine, we know you're out there. If you show yourselves, your friends might live. Try anything foolish . . . and they'll die."

Greg shared a concerned look with Catherine.

"What do we do now?" Catherine asked.

"Exactly as she says." Greg sighed. He lowered his sword, and clutching Catherine's hand, came over the top of the rise.

He found himself in a large clearing. Milady stood at the far side of it. She wore a clean new dress and a devious smile.

The Musketeers, on the other hand, were in considerably worse shape. They had been ambushed. Six swordsmen had laid them flat on their bellies in the center of the clearing and now stood over them, the blades of their weapons resting on the boys' necks.

"Apparently, we should have listened to you," Porthos told Greg.

Aramis and Athos were too stunned to speak. Both just stared at Milady, confused and stunned by her betrayal. Aramis appeared heartbroken, while Athos seethed with anger.

"Drop your sword," Milady told Greg.

Greg saw he didn't have a choice. He let his weapon clatter to the ground. More men emerged from the trees behind him, their blades aimed at him and Catherine.

"D'Artagnan has something else with him," Milady told them. "A magic item of some sort. Check him carefully for it."

Two men forced Greg to the ground. While one pinned him, the other patted him down and quickly came across the Devil's Stone. He held it up to Milady. "Is this what you mean?"

"No, but that's very interesting." Milady crossed the clearing and took the stone. Her eyes glittered as she stared into it. "This must be one half of that Devil's Stone everyone wants so badly. The other half is somewhere in Paris, correct?"

Greg looked to her, surprised.

"Yes, I know all about it," she told him. "I keep my ears open, you see." She tucked the Devil's Stone into the folds of her dress, then spoke to the soldier who'd found it. "The item I'm looking for is a small metal box with strange powers."

Her stooge dutifully frisked Greg and found the phone. He stared at it curiously until Milady demanded, "Bring it to me."

"That's of no use to you!" Greg protested. "Please, I need it. . . ."

"I'm sure you do." Milady took the phone, inspected it curiously, then slipped it into her purse.

"There's no point to any of this," Greg told her. "Face it, Milady, your plans have failed. We've repelled the Spanish army and defeated Dinicoeur. The French army is on its way. You and this small group will be powerless against them."

Milady burst into laughter. "Oh, D'Artagnan, you've been much more alert than your fellow Musketeers. You almost caught me that day at the waterfall. In fact, you would have if you'd realized I wasn't *leaving* a message for the enemy. I was retrieving one."

Greg winced, thinking back to that day at the falls.

Milady hadn't taken anything *out* of her boot. She'd been putting something into it. *If only I'd thought to search her,* Greg thought.

"You were right," Milady continued cruelly. "I *was* plotting against all of you. But not with Dinicoeur. With *him*."

A young man stepped into the clearing. He was around twenty, with curly blond hair and a devilish smirk. He was startlingly handsome, and Milady knew it; she stared at him in the way most men stared at her. "Well done, Milady," he told her. "That went even better than you'd predicted."

He then turned to face the boys, revealing the white rose emblazoned on his tunic. "I suspect you know who I am?"

"Condé," Athos snarled.

"The *Prince* of Condé," he corrected. "The rightful heir to the throne of France."

"We merely took advantage of Dinicoeur's scheme to distract you," Milady explained. "Now, because of the message you sent King Louis, the entire French army is on its way here, leaving Paris vulnerable to attack."

"And you have your own army," Greg said. He felt as though he was standing at the edge of a chasm. He'd just repelled an entire army, defeated Dinicoeur, and regained half the Devil's Stone . . . only to find himself facing another enemy and losing the stone again.

"Yes, I do," Condé said with a smirk. "Thanks to all of you, it will soon conquer Paris—and I will take my rightful place as king of France."

Turn the page for a sneak peek at the final adventure in
the Last Musketeer trilogy . . .

PROLOGUE

Castillon-du-Gard, France
Four hundred miles south of Paris
August 1615

EVEN THOUGH MICHEL DINICOEUR WAS IMMORTAL, HE could still feel pain. And right now, he was in agony. In the four hundred years he'd lived, he'd experienced a great deal of misery—and yet this was the worst so far.

The ordeal he'd been through would have killed a regular man. He'd been shot by flaming arrows, had fallen off a ten-story bridge, and had been swept through a raging river. His flesh was scorched and his bones were fractured. He'd swallowed enough water to drown a fish. During the past few days, he often had wished he could die and end his suffering.

Only one thing kept him going. The desire for revenge.

He would avenge what Greg Rich and the Musketeers had done to him.

The door of the barn where he lay creaked open. Michel recoiled from the sunlight that spilled into the room.

"There's nothing to fear," his own voice told him. "It's only me."

Dominic Richelieu, his younger self, approached. Dominic had rescued Michel from the Gard River and found him this hayloft to hide in while he recovered. As he came to Michel's side, he tried to hide his disgust.

Michel understood why—his face was a hideous mask of scarred flesh—and yet Dominic's reaction made him seethe with anger. "Please tell me you've found something edible this time," he snarled.

"Carrots and beets." Dominic took them from the folds of his clothes.

"Fool!" Michel snapped. "You know I can't eat those things!" Somehow, even his stomach had been affected by the ordeal the Musketeers had put him through. He'd inhaled too much smoke—or maybe too much water—and hadn't been able to keep anything down for days.

"I thought you could try again," Dominic said.

"I need soup," Michel told him. "How hard is it to find

some soup? It's practically all anyone in this cursed time eats!"

"It's not that simple!" Dominic shot back angrily. "We are fugitives, thanks to you! You lost our army, our money, the Devil's Stone . . ."

"None of that was my fault!" Michel roared. "It was the Musketeers!"

"They are only boys, and yet you let the four of them defeat you and our entire army."

"And where were you during all that?"

"Doing exactly what you'd asked of me," Dominic said. "Keeping my distance and letting you handle things. You told me to trust you, that you could take care of everything. You said that under your leadership Paris and all of France would fall. Obviously, I was a fool to believe in you. Everything you have done has led only to failure."

Michel glared at his younger self. "All is not lost. I am healing. By tomorrow, I will be strong enough to travel again. We can make it to Paris."

"In your condition?" Dominic asked. "That will take weeks."

"If I were a mere mortal, perhaps. But I am not." Michel held up his hand as evidence. Although the skin had been badly blistered and burned just days before, it was beginning to return to its normal state. The healing had been much slower than Michel had hoped, but it *was* healing—whereas a normal human would have been scarred for life. "It will not be long before I look just like you again. And while I do not have all my strength back yet, with your help—and a few good horses—we can reach Paris in only a few days."

Dominic frowned in doubt. "And then what? We are wanted men there."

Michel waved his hand dismissively. "The king's guard does not concern me. Once we recover both halves of the Devil's Stone, we will be invincible. The stone, once united, can do the most incredible things."

"And what of the Musketeers?" Dominic asked. "Surely *they* must concern you. They have thwarted your plans twice now."

"They are of no consequence," Michel replied. "I have figured out how to defeat them once and for all."

"You keep saying that—and they keep defeating *us*," Dominic shot back.

Michel suddenly began to laugh. It was a ghastly sound, coming from his burned throat. "But this time will be different. It's a drastic measure, but it won't merely get rid of the Musketeers. . . . It will ensure they never existed at all."

PART ONE

THE
FORTRESS

ONE

Les Baux de Provence
420 miles south of Paris
August 1615

IN LESS THAN A DAY, GREG RICH WOULD DIE.

So would his fellow Musketeers: Athos, Aramis, and Porthos. And Catherine as well. The four stood with him now in the pillory, mocked by passersby.

They were all being held prisoner in the town of Les Baux, a medieval village perched high on a rocky mesa. The village had only one entrance: a steep, narrow road that came up to a heavily fortified gate. Everywhere else, Les Baux was protected by cliffs of limestone that rose hundreds of feet from the swampy lowlands—a fetid, mosquito-ridden maze of marshy bogs. The surrounding mountains were some of the strangest Greg had ever seen, filled with gnarled rock formations.

Although Les Baux was in France, the local lord's allegiance was to the Prince of Condé, not to King Louis XIII. And so the Musketeers, as representatives of King Louis, were to be hung in a public spectacle. Then they would be decapitated. Their heads would be placed on pikes, while their bodies were thrown over the cliffs into the marshland below.

Greg and his friends had been in Les Baux for three days, brought there by Condé's men after Milady de Winter had engineered their capture. They had walked the thirty miles in a single day, forced to slog through the heat without food or rest and with barely any water. The journey had nearly killed Athos. His leg, wounded by an arrow in a surprise attack in Arles, was now swollen and badly infected.

Since arriving, they had spent their nights in cramped, frigid dungeon cells and their days in the pillory. In the town square, they were forced to stand for hours in the blazing sun, hunched over with a wooden frame locked around their wrists and neck, for all the people of Les Baux to see. Jeering townsfolk occasionally threw rotten vegetables at them.

It would have been miserable under any circumstances, but two things made it even worse for Greg.

First, he felt responsible for Catherine being here. He'd had a chance to save her, back at the Pont du Gard when he'd realized his fellow Musketeers were running into a trap. But in the heat of the moment, he hadn't thought to tell her to stay back or run away. Now she would die with them.

Second, he'd lost the trust of Athos and Porthos. He hadn't told them the truth about Michel Dinicoeur—that the man was immortal—until it was too late. Now they knew Greg must have lied to them about himself as well. Both obviously felt deceived, although Athos seemed far more upset. Between his wounded leg and his wounded pride—he'd been stunned when Milady, the woman he loved, had betrayed him—he was seething with anger, and he'd turned that on Greg.

"Athos, Porthos, this is ridiculous," Greg said as they stood in the pillory on the second day. "I've said I'm sorry a hundred times over. I should have been honest with you."

"Then why weren't you?" Porthos demanded.

"Because I was afraid this would be your reaction," Greg admitted. "And the longer I kept secrets from you, the harder it was to tell you. But now I'll tell you anything you want to know. We have to get past this."

"What does it matter?" Athos asked sullenly. "In a day, we'll all be dead."

"Not necessarily," Greg said. "When all of us have worked

as a team, we've done the impossible. We rescued my parents from a prison everyone said was impenetrable. The five of us turned back an entire army. If we put our minds together now, I'm sure we can figure out a way to escape."

Athos frowned in response, but Greg caught a flicker of something in his expression.

"You know it's true, don't you?" Greg asked. "I know that look of yours. You've been trying to work out an escape yourself."

"Of course I have," Athos admitted. "Who wouldn't? I don't want to die."

"Then don't," Aramis said. "You want to know the *real* reason he didn't tell you the truth about himself? I told him not to."

Athos and Porthos shifted their attention to Aramis. "Why?" both demanded.

"Because I didn't think you'd understand," Aramis said. "So if you're going to be angry at anyone, it should be me."

Athos frowned. Greg knew the swordsman was already angry at Aramis; both had vied for the affections of Milady de Winter, before she had betrayed them.

But Porthos gave in. "Who are you, really, D'Artagnan?"

"For one thing, my name isn't D'Artagnan. It's Greg. And I'm not from the Artagnan region of France. I'm from four hundred years in the future."

Porthos and Athos stared at Greg as though he might be insane. Then they looked to Aramis.

"It's true," the cleric told them.

"How is that possible?" Porthos asked.

"Michel Dinicoeur made it happen," Greg told him. "You see, Michel isn't Dominic Richelieu's twin brother. He *is* Dominic Richelieu. At some point in my past—which is actually *your* future—around 1630 or so, Dominic got hold of a magic amulet called the Devil's Stone. The stone is actually two pieces, and when you put them together, they have incredible power. Dominic used that power to make himself immortal and then tried to gain as much wealth as possible. He hoped to live forever as a rich and powerful man, but he was thwarted by the three of you."

Greg fell silent as some townspeople passed, not wanting them to hear his tale. "Down with King Louis!" the people hissed at them. "Death to all who support him!"

"The three of us?" Porthos asked once they were gone. "How?"

"I don't know all the details," Greg said. "But you know how Dinicoeur is missing his right hand? Athos did that to him."

"Well done!" Porthos said to Athos, and Greg thought he saw Athos crack a small smile.

"You all took the Devil's Stone from Dominic and locked him in the Bastille," Greg continued. "The Devil's Stone was broken back in two, and the pieces were separated so they could never be put together again. Meanwhile, Dominic sat in the Bastille for over a hundred years, plotting revenge against you three. Eventually, the Bastille was overthrown during a revolution and Dominic escaped. He changed his name to Michel Dinicoeur and eventually tracked down both pieces of the stone. I don't know where he found the first half, but the second was owned by my family . . . his descendants."

Catherine gasped, her eyes widening. Greg had shared much of his story with her before—but not this part. "You and Richelieu are related?"

Greg nodded. "From what I can tell, I'm his great-great-great-great-great-great-great-grandson. Or something like that. My family was supposed to protect their half of the amulet. Unfortunately, that message got lost over the centuries. Dinicoeur tricked my parents into thinking he was a museum curator at the Louvre in our time, and we brought the amulet to him—"

"Wait," Porthos said. "How could someone be a museum curator at the royal palace?"

"Well," Greg said, "in the future, the Louvre isn't the royal palace. It's a museum; one of the most famous museums in the world."

"If the Louvre is a museum, then where does the king of France live?" Porthos asked.

Greg grimaced, wishing he hadn't opened this can of worms. "There is no king of France anymore," he said.

"You mean France was overthrown?" Porthos gasped.

THE ADVENTURE THAT STARTED IT ALL . . .

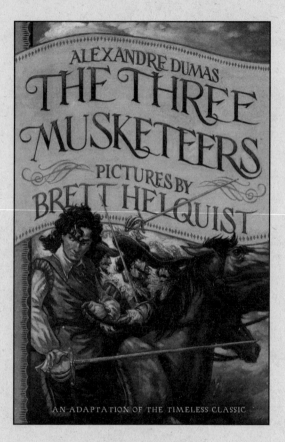

Alexandre Dumas's timeless, swashbuckling tale
takes on a new life in this young readers' edition,
enriched by vibrant illustrations from acclaimed
and bestselling artist Brett Helquist.